Dave The Penguin

By

Nick Sambrook

www.davethepenguin.com

CONTENTS

DEDICATION

This book is dedicated to
Genevieve, Charlie, and Daniel

ACKNOWLEDGMENTS

With love and thanks to Jan
for the creation of this book,
and to Bob Hardy for his inspirational
thoughts and encouragement

1 DAVE THE PENGUIN

Dave was a penguin, not just an ordinary penguin. He was an emperor penguin, and a smart one at that.

He had his evolutionary niche well sorted, and he lived his life on the edge. He was as much of a hermit as you could get, out here in the most remote and extreme part of the Antarctic.

Here it was as far South as it was possible to go, and it wasn't too much of a walk to the sea for the 'lads' fishing trips.

He obviously had all his mates around him, which was good, especially when the weather got a bit much.

He had his 'patch', with his eco-friendly footprints on it, a nice warm coat, a full fish stomach, which he was very proud of, and a responsible job, that of looking after 'the egg'.

When his wife eventually came back, after her several month long hen night party and daytime 'ladies lunches' with the girls, she would always nag him.

"Dave, you can't just stand around all day. Dave, why don't you do this? Dave, why don't you do that? Dave this, Dave that."

Years ago it always used to be an exciting time, noisy, busy, but fun.

Now though, he didn't look forward to her coming home at all. It just wasn't the same as the good old days.

Dave was quite happy though, generally he liked his life, it had always been the same, and every day was just like the next. It was very consistent here, he liked things the same, he liked routine.

It would be, sleep, wake up, think about fish, shuffle, check the egg, and defend it from predators. Which of course there were very few of here - no troublesome snakes, lizards or annoying seagulls to worry about here. Oh No...

Over and over, day after day it was very nice and samey.

He didn't like change, it was 'uncomfortable', 'worrying', 'unsettling' and 'irritating'.

One year however that all changed.

His wife arrived back one day with all the other girls, back from their long annual party. He greeted her with his usual shuffle and raised beak, and she did the same but it didn't last very long. There was something different about her, and she looked like she had something on her mind.

Then before he had a chance to ask her how she was - which would probably have been sometime over the next few days - she interrupted him.

"Dave..." she said "Look, we need to talk. I'm not happy. I'm bored. I've been thinking about this for some time now, and I think we should have a trial separation, just for a while."

Dave shuffled nervously but didn't say anything.

"Being away..." She went on "It's made me realise that life just isn't the same any more. Well to be honest with you Dave, I've changed, and I think we are now just two different penguins you and I. We have become too different from each other now and we want different things.

You just don't seem to understand me anymore. You just don't look at me like you used to, or fancy me, and well you just aren't the same penguin that I married."

Dave looked down.

He looked at the same patch of snow that he had stood on all his life, at the same feet he had always had, the same markings, the same body shape.

He looked up and around, the mountains, the sky, the glacier, they all looked the same too.

He then tried to think of anything else that may have changed. The things he talked about, his limited vocabulary, his routines. He thought about his views on life, his habits, what he did.

No, they were all the same too.

Even his mates, they hadn't changed either.

He got on well with his mates, who were conveniently all called Dave too, which made it so much easier and uncomplicated organising the blokes fishing trips. It also meant he didn't have to think when doing the customary 'Dave' nodded greetings on the way back to his patch again.

"Look Dave…" she went on interrupting his thoughts "It's just that I have met someone else, and well, he makes me happy. He is just like how you used to be, funny, interesting, warm, considerate, passionate, strong, caring.

I just need that at this stage of my life. I just need that bit of excitement again. Honestly you would really like him if you met him."

Dave didn't think he would, but she went on to describe him in more detail anyway, and curiously he sounded just like how Dave thought of himself. In fact, aside from the situation, he would probably have made a good mate to Dave, considering.

He kept looking down and shuffled his feet a bit more.

"It's just that I don't seem to matter to you any more, Dave. Even your friends just know me as 'Dave's wife'. Sometimes I wonder if you even know who I am any more, or care, or even if you remember my name?"

Dave froze, and stopped shuffling.

"Or even if you can remember your own name some days, Dave" she went on.

He started shuffling again. He knew he didn't have a very good memory, but he was fairly sure he would always be OK on that particular one.

"It's just that you never seem to do anything, you just stand around all day. Why don't you invent or build something? Say to protect us from the wind and the cold? Also, I don't feel safe anymore, Dave, I am really worried about polar bears."

She carried on talking, but he didn't hear anything else, he could only cope with a few things in his mind at once. Certain things would take priority, and he was now just thinking about polar bears.

Now Dave had heard about polar bears, he wasn't sure what they were, but he imagined they were large, probably bigger than the glacier, with teeth like a shark. They probably had claws even bigger than his, and dark green scales.

He was good at imagining.

Dave started to become scared, he thought about

what he would have to do, how he would get all his mates together.

He was worried now, what would they do? He was sure he would recognise one if he saw it. It made him shiver, which was odd because it wasn't even cold.

He always seemed to think of lots of confusing things when his wife was around.

He shuffled some more, his eyes going back and forth looking at the footprints in front of him trying to work it all out, trying to solve the problem….

"**DAVID !**" she shouted. He jumped, and looked up at her.

"You aren't listening to me again, David!"

"It's OK, It's OK" said Dave, startled "Err yes, I understand, it's fine, it's fine."

"You do?" his wife exclaimed, taken aback. Her face then started to smile around her beak, and she nodded up and down excitedly.

"That's so wonderful, I was so worried you would be cross and upset."

"No,' said Dave "it's fine. I understand everything. OK bye then…" he said blankly.

There was a long pause.

His wife's expression would have changed if she wasn't a penguin.

"Well…" she said "I have to say you are being very grown up about all of this. I was expecting you to be angry, begging me to stay, and telling me how you will change, and try to make it all work."

"No" said Dave. "It's fine, it's simple. As you say, you have changed, you want different things in life, you want me to be something else, to change too, but also to be the same penguin that you first met. You are not happy, even though I am, and you want me to be happy being someone different."

"Well…" said his wife confused "Well err, yes, I suppose that's all true…" she said. "I have to say Dave that I am really surprised. I thought you would be really angry and upset. My friends, when I told them what I was going to do, said that I should just do it anyway, and go off without telling you. However I didn't want to just do that, I didn't think it was right. They have been trying to get me to do this for ages."

"That's strange," said Dave "three of them came and said 'Hello' a few hours before you arrived back and they didn't say anything. In fact they seemed quite pleased to see me."

His wife looked even more confused, and a few creases appeared on her forehead.

"So," said Dave "the only thing that has changed here - and the only thing that isn't happy - is you. You are in effect a modifying chaotic variable force, an agent provocateur, trying to invoke motion on a controlling static mass in equilibrium, in an attempt to effect evolutionary change in the mind of a collective macro-organism."

There was another very long pause, and his wife looked at him suspiciously.

"Have you been watching those natural history documentaries again Dave?" She asked him accusingly, with her eyes narrowed.

"No, it's much more complex than that. I am actually a male program life form in a minimally effectible device, projected by my mind which is a static evolutionary harmonized bubble, that has decided that paradise is just life without change. I am several thousand years old. I am Dave of the clan Dave, and I am immortal. So I do not want to change, and I am very happy with things as they are."

His wife just stood there with her beak open, unable to say anything.

"We have also perfected the cloning process too" he went on, "and are able to reproduce female penguins so they are the exact copy of the originals with no latency errors. Do you see that penguin over there? The one walking this way? She is a clone of you, and has been programmed to be my next wife."

His wife immediately turned around to look, and she saw to her horror a young female penguin who was exactly the same as she had been twenty years earlier.

Exactly, with all the attitude, energy, looks and confidence that she once had.

"This process…" continued Dave "happens every twenty years just to remind me of all the effort I am saving. All the work, energy, thinking and change, to aid in the evolution and learning of the collective consciousness mind thing. It's also necessary as even though I would be perfectly happy with you as you are for eternity, you are the one that is made to change by external collective forces, and there is nothing we can do about that, it's just part of nature. It's what you are driven to do. But please don't worry about me, honestly I will be fine."

There was another long pause, and his horrified wife looked at him in shock.

"I can't believe you are doing this to me…" she said "after all we have been through."

"I haven't done anything" said Dave, "I haven't changed, I am exactly the same, and I have been for many thousands of years. Besides I thought you were the one that wanted to leave? I was just making you feel better about it. Honestly go, I will be fine with the new keener, younger, energetic you. I am sure she can do all the same things you used to do for me, and I am sure she will carry on looking after me. Don't even think twice about it."

Then she started to cry. A lot.

"It's no good" said Dave "you can't try and invoke an emotional response in me, I am an immovable male object."

"Please, please…" she sobbed, "I love you Dave, I don't want this to happen."

The young version of his wife walked up to them, and then carried on walking past, and completely ignored them. His wife suddenly looked very confused, and turned to Dave.

"But I thought you said…." she started to ask, but he raised his wing to stop her from saying anything else.

"It's OK," he said "we go through this whole process every twenty years, it's fine. I love you just the way you are, it's perfectly OK. I love you as you were, and I will always love you. We are both perfectly happy; it is just something else that is trying to invoke change."

Then in that instant a preprogramed subroutine kicked in, and she changed to look just as she had twenty years ago, and so did Dave, although in his mind he still looked the same.

He still had the same amazing 45kg of toned physique, and the same good looks as he always had.

After all it was hard to re-sculpt perfection.

She was still sobbing slightly but was recovering well, the full enormity of what was going on gradually sinking in. After a while their memories would go back twenty years again to when they first met, which in Dave's case didn't take very long for the data files to be deleted and reset.

Their programs would start again and they would be happy, with no memory of the last twenty years. Several moments later she turned to him and smiled, slightly disorientated.

"Hello," she said "what's your name?"

"It's Dave" said Dave.

"Dave…" she repeated "That's a nice name."

Suddenly Dave had a weird feeling, it was as if he had been here before.

A sort of 'Dave-ja-vu', moment.

Then it was gone.

"Here," said Dave "you can have this egg, it's just a ceramic one with a small nuclear powered heater inside, we use it to keep our feet warm. I am just off fishing with the lads, I will be back in a few months…" and with that he waddled off to the sea, leaving his wife happy again for the next twenty years.

Well that was the idea anyway.

After all, what more could you want in life?

2   DAVE SAVES THE DAY

Even though he was a penguin, Dave knew that his body was just a programmable biological device.

It was fairly obvious really when you thought about it, which of course he did, quite a lot of the time.

After all, out here on the ice, what else was there to do, especially if you were a smart and inquisitive penguin?

Which of course he was.

Out here on the ice plateau everything was very simple, black and white as it were, just penguins and ice, so things became obvious without all the other clutter and complications that existed elsewhere.

His wife had been away for a few weeks now, so he had plenty of time to stand quietly, to ponder on the bigger questions, to just contemplate things, well of what few things there were around anyway.

For example, he knew that he knew about things now that he didn't know when he was a chick, and he had seen and done many things that he hadn't done then.

He could remember them; remembered doing them, seeing things, and working things out. So somehow all that information, all that knowing, all that 'experience', had all got into him, or more to the point into his mind, somehow.

Even though no one had actually told him anything, no one had explained anything, and he hadn't read anything, somehow he just 'knew'.

Equally when he was a chick, he knew things that he didn't know when he was an egg. He could hardly remember anything from when he was an egg.

Dave looked down at his feet at the new egg he was standing over at the moment. He also remembered that as a chick he could 'do' a lot more things than he could do as an egg; equally he could understand things a lot better, and he was much more interesting in a 'doing and moving around' sort of way.

Yet nobody seemed to be interested or bothered or concerned as to how that change had happened; that growing from practically nothing into something that knew how to peck, waddle, slide, eat fish, and swim.

All without the help or guidance of say a penguin manual, or training lessons, or school. So it was obvious to Dave that everything was built up from programs, which you just picked up, from somewhere, that somehow got into your head.

It was as if right from the start you were tuned into some penguin radio at a specific frequency, with all the knowing stuff in there like a story, that told your evolving mind how to build a penguin.

All the instructions and knowledge were there to download just like on Penguintube, you just had to use the right resonating search term, and choose the most popular or highly rated instruction video, that didn't leave you with too many spare screws and parts left over at the end.

What wasn't obvious to Dave though, was how it all got there, and where it all came from. All that 'knowing' stuff; all that 'how' and 'what' you should be type of information.

He knew it didn't all come from penguin DNA, that 1.5 gigabytes of data mostly went into describing what a penguin should be; its physicality, shape, nature, colours, body parts and all that stuff.

You could barely define a robot penguin with just that. Perhaps it was a sort of booting program, that loaded everything else up, from somewhere, linked to other things that worked out a way forward, figured out what worked and what didn't, that sort of thing.

Dave was very proud of his DNA, he had spent a long time working on it, refining it to the level of perfection that it was today. But it didn't have anything in there about how to recognise fish types, swim after them and catch them, how to dive, or how to walk with a waddle.

Nobody had even mentioned fish when he was a chick,, and he hadn't seen any films with them in either. But as soon as he got into the water and saw some, he knew what they were, and what to do; it was all instinct whatever that was, and wherever it came from. He already knew which ones were good to eat, and how to catch them.

He even knew which ones would try to eat him, and ones he had to swim away from, like the ones with big teeth, and whiskers, and black flippers that could come out of the sea to get you.

Or the dreaded giant black and white fish, with the big tall fin that had with glossy skin and wide mouth and sharp teeth and sneezed a lot.

He hated those type of fish, they made him very 'nervous'.

It was also a mystery as to how his cells knew what they had to do; they all had the same DNA, even though 95% of it was 'junk' as far as he was concerned, but that seemed a bit odd considering how amazingly efficient he was, so what all that extra 'junk' was all used for was a mystery.

Somehow his cells knew what function they had, where they had to be and what they had to do in different parts. Who had told them all of that? Where had that information come from, all that knowing stuff, and what was right and what was wrong?

It was like the junk DNA was some sort of bootstrap program that downloaded all the information it needed from a cloud drive somewhere, which itself evolved over time both from his perspective and from the collective penguin mind, which meant that part of him was part of it, evolutionarily speaking.

Dave looked at his body again. *Whatever it was, was pretty smart, and with a good eye for style* he thought.

He knew that basic life forms like algae used up nearly all their DNA programming on just being what they were, but then they didn't need to fish or dance. But the idea for algae DNA must have come from somewhere originally, perhaps the planet got the idea from somewhere in a sort of dream.

He saw a patch of algae on a rock next to him, he scratched it with his foot and bits of it fell onto the snow. *There* thought Dave, *that showed it*. It made him feel better; it was good to know there was always something 'below' him in the evolutionary pecking order.

The trouble now though was that he had upset the balance, he was forcing it to evolve, in ten million years it might evolve to be a bigger penguin with teeth, and 'get' him. Worriedly he covered over the patch of algae that had fallen to the ground with some snow, and hoped nobody had noticed.

However he also knew that there *were* things he had actually learnt as he was growing up – things like shuffling. He had picked that habit up from his Dad, who used to do it when his Mum shouted at him.

It was a sort of programmed response, so Dave did the same, especially when he was shouted at. It was just the thing you did. He also used to arch his back when he put his feet into very cold water, which was quite a lot of the time.

He had seen his Dad do that too, and that is why he did the same. He just copied it, and did it without thinking now. It like sneezing loudly, he didn't have to, it was just what he did. But he wasn't sure why.

It was a total mystery. All that stuff had come from somewhere, some strange mysterious, all knowing thing that he couldn't see. Even skills that he had like his unfailing sense of direction, his migratory urge and amazing sex drive.

That had come from somewhere too, something that stored things collectively, for everyone, everything, all in one place. He looked down at the egg again between his feet and shuffled. He then looked back up into the sky at the colours swirling and changing high in the sky, almost as if it were alive.

He had to come up with a better descriptive term than 'collective penguin mind', he couldn't use terms like 'hive mind' or 'herd mentality', and as they didn't fly, 'flock' was no good either. 'Colony' sounded too much like ants to him, and it made him itch every time he thought about it.

Besides penguins sort of huddled and bunched together, but that didn't fit either, and it also didn't really help describe technically what it was either.

His brain was starting to hurt now. This was tough going - so he tried to think of something else.

He looked up at the psychedelic lights in the sky and he thought of the song –

Lucy in the Sky with Diamonds.

He then thought of Lucy from

The Lion, the Witch and the Wardrobe;

he liked that book series; it had been one of his favourites until he had lent them to someone and they hadn't ever returned them. The trouble was he couldn't remember who he had lent it to.

Mind you the films were never as good as his imagination. The same had happened with his *Pinocchio* DVD, he liked that film too, especially Jiminy Cricket, and the Blue Fairy, he wished he had a blue fairy.

He wondered what had happened to it, or indeed Pinocchio himself, perhaps he had been made into a wardrobe, or a cupboard under the stairs. His mind had lots of things coming in all together; DNA, Pinocchio as an under stairs cupboard, Lucy, the Blue Fairy, and Scarlet Johannsson.

He was now busy building up a synchronistic mind map in his head; you know one of those things with thought bubbles and lines connecting them.

He put them all down in some structure until he

was happy with it, with him in the centre. Now, in his mind, he started drawing pictures in the Scarlet Johannsson bubble, and moved it closer to the middle, and threw a bucket of iced water over the *Pinocchio* one.

Concentrate! Dave thought, *Concentrate!*

Focus on the now, don't let your mind wander!

But while he was on the subject, he remembered that he had been worried about his sex drive earlier in the year.

It had been such a long time since he had seen his wife, and he had completely forgotten how he was supposed to feel. It had become a sort of distant memory now, a vague idea.

It had worried him, he had even taken to watching some natural history documentaries, to sort of get himself 'back in the mood' and that type of thing, but it hadn't worked.

It was difficult to show love in a documentary, and it wasn't something he could talk to his mates about. He had tried that once and it was just met with weird looks and uncomfortable coughing.

He had worried that he was eating the wrong sort of fish, or not getting enough exercise, but a quick look at his amazing physique reassured him that it was certainly not any of these things.

He had told himself that it must have been that he had just forgotten the program in his head, or it was very slow to be loaded, nothing to do with him at all; just bad or inefficient programming, or slow functionality.

So he had been determined that when she came

back that she wouldn't get the wrong idea; that she wouldn't think he was going 'off' her and not loving her any more, that he was still fit and healthy and virile. That he was still a fully functioning, switched on, real 'bloke' type of penguin.

It had taken her somewhat by surprise.

He looked down at the egg again.

But it didn't say anything, nor did it shake its head disapprovingly, but then it didn't have to.

Dave wondered if it was going to be a boy or a girl penguin. If it was a boy he could take it on fishing trips and teach it things. He tried to think of a name for it, he thought for a while, 'Dave' seemed like a good choice.

Penguins didn't have surnames; they didn't need them, besides they were very pretentious, like 'Livingstone'. Then again if it was going to be a girl then he would have to think of something else, he could almost visualise her looking at him expectantly, waiting for him to do something, make a decision, just like her mother did.

Girl penguins seemed to know a lot more than boy penguins, he thought, *they seemed to know the game from day one, like they were pre-programmed to know things in a way that boy penguins weren't. It isn't very fair,* thought Dave.

Then again that was the way it was, the way it had to be, and who said life and nature had to be fair?

He decided to wait and see what happened and worry about it later.

Yes that was probably best.

Dave wondered if he himself had any control over the programming that went into what was going on inside the egg. Could he shape it, affect it in some way, influence it?

If it was all one big overall program that controlled everything, one giant operating system, could he change things, direct things, shape what was decided, dictate how everything turned out? Or was it all predetermined, set in place, fate, governed by set rules, and there was nothing you could do about it, and it would all be what it would be?

But that didn't seem right, the thought of everything being predetermined didn't seem correct. If that was the case, anything he did wouldn't make any difference, and what would be the point of that?

He may as well not be there at all or just be a rock. What point would there be in him being there at all? What was his purpose? If he couldn't change things or influence things, there would be no point in anything.

Whatever it was that had created everything could have just made everything as it would have been at the end of things, as they say on his favourite cook shows – "Here is one I prepared earlier…"

He looked down at his feet and shuffled a little on the ice to keep his feet warm.

Somehow though he felt involved in a process, part of a larger system - one in balance, in harmony, synchronised, growing, evolving, or at least that was the idea.

What he did and thought made a difference; it must do, affecting the overall direction to some extent, in some conscious way.

Obviously there were winners and losers in the process, all forming parts of a system that was there to work something out, to be something, grow, learn, achieve something; something BIG.

Yet at the same time it was trying to preserve something, something at the lowest levels, from the bottom up, otherwise it could have just been created, all outright in its final form, without the need to grow, adapt, and evolve. Even if it was very hit and miss.

He shuffled some more, and his eyes darted back and forth around the gritty snow in front of him. This was all getting intellectually very deep.

Dave wondered if his other penguin mates had thought about the same problem, but he suspected that they didn't think much at all, about anything, except ice, snow, fish, light, dark, storms and of course polar bears.

Yet no other penguins could see things the way he saw them. They couldn't see things from his perspective, but then nobody knew what he knew, yet did that matter anyway? Other penguins knew things he didn't, and saw the world differently, that was fine too.

There was no point in trying to explain his perspective of everything to everyone else, they just wouldn't understand, or appreciate it, and they would probably think he was mad anyway.

It made him worry though. About everything. Things were just not right, overall, there were a lot of things that 'needed sorting out', 'resolving' to stop him worrying about things. He just didn't know what they were.

There was that polar bears thing again, back in his head. He had thought about it again and now he just couldn't get it out of his head.

His wife had mentioned it a few months ago, and it was nagging at him again. Also there was that thing he had just thought about too, that 'Why are we here?' thing, that was there too in the same way, annoying, irritating, a sort of itchy mental feeling in his head, like a note out of harmony in the song in the world, and a pluck on the string in the music of the universe.

Dave liked the universe. He would look up at it in the middle of the night, in the harsh cold pitch blackness when the sun was away - when you could see all the far off tiny lights in the sky.

He liked that time the best; it was peaceful, it made him feel humble, small, insignificant, and yet not so, as if he were what it was all there for, and that he was an important part of it and on some journey within it.

It made him feel like singing some nights. Well almost.

Dave was good at singing, he had a great voice, just as did all his mates. He knew it was a gift, a program that had come from somewhere, and not from his Mum or Dad that was for sure, but it must have been sent to him by something that wasn't him.

Some days he loved to sing out loud and clear, and even his wife would comment at how loud and 'nice' it was.

He could dance too; he had amazing rhythm. He practised dancing a lot, and had shown his wife some of his moves, but she had just laughed and fallen on the floor, but he realised now that she was just jealous.

He wondered how she had learnt to recognise things that were funny, where the programming had come from for that, but clearly some programs weren't perfect, there were errors here and there. He found lots of things funny, or at least he used to, especially when he was a chick.

He wondered if some programs were fixable. What was humour if it wasn't a program? Just slightly different with everyone, or was it a sense like smell or taste?

Why were so many things bothering him? It was a lot for a simple penguin to take in, a lot to think about all in one go. Also why did he feel so responsible, with such a need to do something about it all, to sort all the problems out, and save everyone from polar bears?

He knew nothing of the real world, how it looked , how it worked, what it all meant, so why did he had this driving urge to save it, and what was it all to him anyway? Why did he care?

Dave had memories.

He could remember all of his past lives, which in fairness were pretty much all the same as this one.

The same patch of snow, same glacier, same sea, same sky, same fish, and the same routines.

He could remember everything that he had seen, the places he had been to, all he had known, all the experiences he had had, and all of the world he had been in.

He could also remember all the other penguins he had met; names, faces and events over thousands of years. As a result he was now a masterpiece of refined evolutionary engineering; a honed program of perfection, modified and developed over thousands of years, to be pretty much the same as he always was.

With all that knowledge though came great responsibility - he remembered that phrase from a film he had once seen. This time around though something different had occurred, or something had reached a point of change, some point of criticality, something important. He wondered what it was.

Dave knew about the collective penguin mind, combined together with an overall driving force. He knew about things happening for no apparent reason, things all changing in one go at the same time for some inexplicable reason, like everyone deciding to go fishing all at the same moment.

Who had made that choice? He certainly never had, and none of his mates had 'fessed up to having come up with the idea on their own, and yet everyone suddenly started moving at the same time like some sort of switch being pressed, some collective thought occurring naturally like some involuntary group decision being made all at the same time.

It was like some sort of invisible instant voting system that no one else could actually see.

Yet, surprisingly, everything was generally all fine, everything worked OK, as long as there was nothing wrong, but he had this nagging feeling in the back of his mind that there was a fundamental problem, something big, something that was going wrong with the world.

However, perhaps there was always something wrong, and he was just normally not aware of it, or bothered enough by it to actually care. He was just a simple penguin after all, so how could he change anything, what could he do about it all, and what real difference could he make?

Even if he could, what if he made the wrong choice, gave the wrong ideas, made the wrong suggestions to whatever this thing was that did all the programming, the decision making, the voting? How would it all end up?

Dave didn't want that level of responsibility.

He was not designed for such big ideas, for big thoughts, on big problems. How could anything listen to such a small voice, it must know far more than he did anyway, and in any case how would it benefit him? It had never done anything for him.

He stood there on the ice sheet and felt just like a small black dot in a vast expanse of white, trying to get the thoughts clear in his head. A small bead of sweat appeared on his brow, trickled along his forehead, along his beak, and formed a tiny ice crystal at the end.

Two weeks passed.

In the morning of that fateful day everyone felt it. A change in the information in the air. A sense of something coming. A feeling. There was clearly a storm on its way, everyone knew it.

Even though nothing was visibly different, everyone could sense what was coming; the change in pressure, the smell on the air, the nervous vibrational tension.

The clouds in the sky looked different too; they moved faster and had different shapes.

Everyone started to get agitated, and it got very noisy, the peace and harmony of the colony was gone.

Later that morning things still hadn't improved,

and some penguins had started to huddle together, and others were heading off to the sea along the defined paths.

Dave had always thought it odd that everyone followed the same paths, until he tried being 'different' one day, and went 'of road', a rebel penguin, and ended up stuck down in a crevasse for two hours, alone until heads appeared above from penguins who had followed his new path.

God that had been really embarrassing.

He tried to concentrate. Something was definitely wrong with this situation; there was a 'not right' feeling in the air - and in his mind.

The sea seemed to be the wrong place to be heading towards, it wasn't safe, but he didn't know why. A few fights had broken out, and groups were forming, each competing with each other over what to do, where to stand and who should stand at the front or the back.

Even eggs were starting to be abandoned as penguins began to wander off on their own; everyone was trying to work out what to do.

Dave's head was buzzing. It felt under pressure, busy, and it ached, as if there was a lot going on in there.

Dave stood on his own. He closed his eyes and concentrated.

It was dark… that always surprised him for some reason.

He concentrated his mind some more, focused, and allowed the blackness to deepen and his imagination to live within it, to see where it took him.

He expanded his mind, and tried to get his head around the whole world, becoming mindful of everything.

He put himself into the world perspective, into the collective mind's eye, and thought big thoughts - and big thoughts came back.

It was a surprise, both to him, and the thing that he was trying to get his head and mind around.

Nothing had ever done that before, but then you had to know what you were dealing with to be able to communicate with it, to perceive it, and then interface with it.

Like with anything, you can't see something if you aren't looking at it. It also helped if you knew what it was, and how it thought then you also had a reasonable chance of getting its attention.

It wasn't like talking to a glacier, Dave had tried that, this had something alive as part of it. Glaciers were different, even though they moved, they weren't alive.

Glaciers also just took ages to say anything, and weren't interested in him; they were just full of complaining creaks and groans.

However, what he was communicating with now wasn't like a penguin's mind at all; it was bleak, cold, harsh, and very 'big' and 'complex'.

It was only communicating with him now as it needed information, help. It was worried about something, something coming, a problem. But it couldn't see, it couldn't understand what it was or put it in context with Dave's perception of the world.

It just knew there was fear, a threat. It had no real

way of being able to describe or perceive what was happening, like a chick inside a giant egg that had sensed something. Fear.

Yet Dave could see, and understand. He knew what had to happen, and his thoughts, mind, and knowledge merged with this bigger thing. He worked out what was being 'said' and what was around him, what was coming and what needed to happen, all at the same time.

Dave now thought of himself as a program rather than as a penguin, a functional part of something bigger.

He had knowledge that he had to pass on. The thing that was bigger than him was worried too, probably because all the things that it was made up of were worried.

Yet it couldn't see or understand why.

Dave knew what to do though. Dave had a plan, and the bigger thing knew what Dave was thinking.

Between him and it, something was 'worked out' and then it went away, and something changed.

With the information that Dave had exchanged he now knew that there was a giant storm coming; probably the worst one ever in history. It would be full of violent winds, dark clouds, blizzards, the worst conditions imaginable.

They all would not survive it.

The sky in the distance was already turning black, and the wind was getting stronger. Winds here were not at all friendly, they were very violent, and they carried ice that blinded and bit like beaks. They were unimaginably fast, and could lift a penguin up into the sky, and you would never see them again, or ever know where they had gone to.

Dave opened his eyes and a thousand pairs of eyes were looking at him, directly at him, expectantly.

Then as one, at the same time, and with one mind, all the other penguins started shuffling together towards a cliff on the side of the glacier. The cliff was facing away from the wind, it was somewhere protected where they would all be safe as long as they all stuck together.

The penguins that had set off towards the sea now all stopped too, and turned and headed back to the main group. It was as if an overriding program had kicked in, and they were all now following new instructions, new guidance.

Within half an hour they were all huddled up underneath the side of the glacial cliff, just as the snow and wind started to build up around them.

They would be safe. Directed by a set of coordinated thoughts and ideas, focused out of necessity for survival.

The storm was horrific, growing worse by the hour, the noise was like a thousand polar bears all roaring at once, but they were all safe, sheltered on the right side of the cliff.

The snow flurries billowed around them, and settled all around them, and drifted over them. Everyone was terrified and all they could do was huddle closer together. Occasionally funnels of spinning winds would pass over the plain where they had been standing before;

Dave had seen these funnels before in a film. They

would have been sucked up by the tornado, off to the Land of Oz where there were lots of strange animals, long roads, and people that sprayed themselves orange.

The winds were indescribably fast and lasted for hours into the night, and they only died down when the sun came up the following morning and only then did they all begin to climb out of the snow

Where their nesting area had been was now several feet deep in snow. If they had stayed where they had been they would not have made it. The seas in the distance were just a mass of froth.

Everyone climbed out of the drifts and shook themselves clear of snow and slowly waddled back to where they had come from to get back to normality, and resume the daily routines on the nesting grounds.

All except Dave. Dave was exhausted. His feet felt as heavy as rocks, and he ached. He was so shattered he couldn't move. His head hurt, especially on the top, and he couldn't think very clearly. It was as if he had been running or swimming all night whilst doing lots of very tricky sums all at the same time.

He just couldn't move, he just wanted to go back to sleep.

Eventually he managed to climb out of the snow and walk slowly with the egg still balanced on his feet, slowly making his way back to the nesting ground.

He felt so weary, so drained, exhausted, which was odd as he hadn't actually *done* anything, yet thoughts and ideas were raging through his mind.

He just needed sleep, but he needed to get back, and he shuffled slowly, head down, back to the nesting area on his own.

When he finally arrived back, he looked up. Someone had stolen his patch.

He recognised the intruder straight away. Dave had had problems with this one before. It was a stupid, selfish penguin, who was full of himself. He wasn't as big or strong or as good looking as Dave but he was a few years younger, and he had a mean sneer.

Dave didn't know his name, and he didn't care, he wasn't one of his mates. His name probably wasn't 'Dave' either, he didn't like him, and his name was probably something stupid anyway.

He felt the programming change in his body, new programming was instinctively coming in, starting up functions like adrenaline, angry face, bodily inflation, and fight or flight – which in Dave's case left only one option. His personality was changing - he could feel it - just as a dogs did when they had a raw bone; things kicked in and hypnotised him to be in a different state; something else.

Dave was tired though, far too exhausted to put up a fight. The other penguin eyed him up as Dave waddled up, and then gave him that indignant 'I don't know what you mean - this isn't yours' look, then a 'What are you going on about?' look, followed by the aggressive 'What are you going to do about it anyway?' one.

But Dave didn't have the energy to fight for what was his, he was shattered and even the act of resistance and the adrenaline rush has exhausted him to his bones.

Sometimes life could be so unfair, it was direct

injustice after all he had done - but then that was the way it was, he could not fight, not today anyway, but then tomorrow was another day and he would have all his energy and strength back.

His dropped his head down to the ground and turned away. Poor Dave.

He looked around at all his penguin mates, but they all seemed to be back to normal, acting as if nothing had happened, like the storm had never occurred, as if everything was just the same as it always had been. It was as if all the programs had just restarted again from where they had left off the day before the storm, just the same as if nothing had happened. Nobody seemed to care about him or what had gone on.

Dave imagined it would be just the same in a thousand years' time, or ten thousand; nothing changing, day after day. He thought about trying to explain what he had done or what had happened to them, but he knew it was pointless.

The only thing that seemed to have changed was that he was exhausted. And he had lost his patch. They all seemed to just get on with things, and behaved as if nothing had happened, like it had all been a dream. Everything was as it had been before, and if anything they were just ignoring Dave altogether, with a 'what are you on about attitude?'

Life was so unfair. Why did he bother, and what was the point of it all?

He walked off slowly with the egg on his feet to the far edge of the group, past lots of other penguins that eyed him suspiciously and defensively as he went.

Finally he reached the lesser priority nesting

patches, where he just stood alone; cold and tired and weak.

He stood for a long while thinking.

If everyone were all programs thought Dave, *what difference does it make, all of this, and does it matter anyway?*

Somehow Dave thought that it did, he thought it must do for some reason. He tried to get some sleep, to rest, to get his energy back up again.

No one would ever know it was Dave that had done this, and so nobody would thank him, or even show any sign of being grateful, so what was the point?

He may as well just behave like everyone else, look after 'Number One'. The only consolation or reward was that he was alive, along with everyone else.

At the time it just seemed the right thing to do. He just saw what had to be done, answered the questions, and did what he thought was right, as would anyone. That didn't make him feel any better though. Now that he was suffering and being badly treated and ignored that didn't seem right or fair.

Several hours later all the girls arrived back. They had sensed something had occurred, and that they needed to get back for some reason.

They all arrived in waves, and the greetings came in noisy calls and beak waving.

As Dave looked up the slope to the middle of the colony he could see that the penguin that had taken Dave's patch in the middle was being greeted by several interested single attractive girl penguins, and he was now raising his beak and puffing out his chest as if he were top penguin, trying every p-p-pick-up trick going.

Dave liked him even less now, and tried to work out what his name could be, and he managed to come up with several suitable ideas. Dave looked away.

It was late evening now, almost dark. The wind dropped to a light breeze, and the remaining clouds cleared.

The coloured swirling lights in the South sky came through, illuminating all the penguins in different colours, and the ground around them, with vibrant flashing reds, greens, and blues.

Dave turned to the North, and saw in the distance a female penguin coming towards him along the ice on her own.

In this light she looked blue, a sort of pale sapphire or turquoise aquamarine colour surrounded her. He had seen some stones that colour on a beach somewhere.

It was difficult to see in the fading light but that's what it looked like, like she was glowing blue.

His wife came up to him and greeted him calmly with a knowing smile on her face as if she understood everything that had gone on, everything that had happened, everything that he had done.

Which of course Dave knew was impossible. But she could tell something was not quite right with him so she just cuddled up to him, and rested her head over his shoulder.

She didn't say anything, and neither did Dave. But he was happy. He felt warm inside now, and stronger every minute.

He hugged his wife and tears began to roll down

his cheeks. He wasn't sure why he was crying, he didn't know what it was for.

Was it relief, sadness, happiness? He didn't know, he just had tears; it was something he had no control over, or something he had ever experienced before, they just flowed out and landed on the yielding snow.

But there were still these bigger problems in his mind, still there. What could he possibly do?

He was just a simple penguin, what could he do to save everyone, what possible difference could he make to it all?

He just stood there and hugged his wife again, and she closed her eyes, the egg safely held on his feet between them gave a slight tapping noise.

The thoughts and worries he had disappeared, it was all OK again, nothing else mattered, he closed his eyes too and everything was as it should be.

The camera pulled back from looking down on the two penguins. It zoomed out away from the white glacial plateau domain.

As it panned out, the large colony was now just a small dark smudge on the edge of the icepack which was breaking up slowly into pieces and floating off.

It zoomed back further to show the continent and the iceberg filled seas around it, back, and back, and back, until it took in the whole World from outer space.

It was just a simple blue-green disc with cities, countries, seas, aircraft, clouds, ocean liners, and storms.

From here, everything was much bigger, much more complicated, sophisticated, and difficult.

Yet when you looked at it from here it was also just as simple as an isolated colony of penguins on a remote glacial ice sheet.

Dave's world, his life, his environment, were simple, uncomplicated, isolated, straightforward and well defined on this icy plateau.

Yet it formed just a single piece of a vast complex puzzle that was our world. He had no thoughts of the sphere he was on, its vast organisations, structures, or knowledge that had formed into protected academic shapes.

He had no understanding of words like zeitgeist, macro-organism, or collective consciousness, or even how to construct a programme on how it all should evolve into an integrated self-aware form.

No, all that would have been far too much for Dave to cope with, yet the underlying nature and ideas required were surprisingly very simple.

It was just all common sense stuff really, things which Dave was very good at, things that just needed bravery and faith to come into play for himself, and everyone.

So in response to Dave's question - on what difference could he make to it all....

..The answer was, surprisingly, quite a lot,
   and on a scale he couldn't possibly imagine!.

Dave was a penguin on the edge.

His wife had told him he looked stressed and worried. She was concerned about how tired and weary he was after the storm had passed, and all he had been through.

With all the issues with his patch having to be retaken and keeping off rivals it had taken its toll on him. She had said it had all made him irritable and a bit short with her too, but he was fairly sure he was still the same height as he had always been.

His friends had told him he that he really needed to 'Chill out', and then sniggered. "Mate," they said "you need to stay cool" and then fell about laughing. But he didn't think it was very bloody funny.

He had tried to explain to his wife what had happened, and what he had done, but he didn't have the words, and she either wasn't interested or didn't understand.

Somehow though she seemed to believe him, and know, but she still wasn't impressed or willing to acknowledge or talk about it for some reason. She seemed to know what he had done, and what he was, and what had happened, but in a different way. However, she was more interested in day to day things, getting on with things.

It is very odd, thought Dave, but he let it go.

A few days later he was still no better, so she had told him to go off and think about things, take a bit of time to find himself, and she took over the job of looking after the egg while he went off…. Far off.

So now he stood on his own way out on the glacier and shuffled a little closer to the edge, and peered over the ice cliff where a large section of it had broken off in the recent storm.

Where he was now standing had all originally sloped gently down to the sea, but now all that was left was a cliff, a steep drop and the sea at the bottom, and no way of getting to it safely without a long walk around.

You just had to accept it, these environmental things, treat them as 'part of life', and work around them. Move on, and come to terms with the change. Being this close to the edge, and one step away or one icefall from certain death, certainly put things into perspective though; made things clearer as to what was important, and what was not.

It brought into sharp focus what life really meant, what it was all about, and why he thought the way he did.

Dave wasn't complaining though - unlike the ice beneath his feet, which was now making ominous groaning and creaking sounds. Which was odd, as he didn't think that his light frame would make any difference.

Dave had just come to look at the view and to explore, not to fish this time.

He had brought his new tape player and headphones that his wife had given him for his birthday, to give him something to listen to, to keep him busy while she had been away.

He was currently listening to *Heaven Can Wait* by Meatloaf. He liked that song, it was as if the lyrics were written for him, *but then you could say that about most songs* he thought, and it would probably apply to most penguins, and they probably all felt the same way too.

He liked listening and thinking and watching far away things.

When the tape finished he looked through his bag for some other tapes he had found washed up on the beach that morning. One caught his eye - it read…

'Meditation for Self Help – Extreme (under the counter version)'

Dave didn't think he needed any help, he felt fine, relaxed and very calm. He looked at the back of the tape; it read ..

'If you are on the edge – you can use this tape to learn to access all the levels of your mind, and unleash the powers within you for greater understanding, a better more relaxed calmer you, and a better happier world'.

He thought it was odd that a tape knew where he was, what he was doing, and what he had to do. But then life was full of surprises, and with Dave, things seemed to arrive at the right time, and be there when they had to, and say what they needed to say.

He was sure his wife said the same about him.

Dave was a bit sceptical about these sort of self-help spiritual things; he only believed in what he could see, touch, and hear or smell.

He was the sort of penguin that liked to call a spade a spade, if he had one, which of course he didn't.

Just in the same way that he wasn't having a mid-life crisis, because if he was he would admit it, obviously.

He had tried to use a meditation tape that he had borrowed from a friend about a year ago, but it hadn't worked very well. He remembered the start of it telling him to close his eyes and relax, let his mind wander, and then suddenly it shouted at him rudely "...FIVE!! – NOW WIDE AWAKE - FEELING FINE...." which startled him badly.

He had a whole hour of his life missing somewhere, a sore throat, he was dribbling from his beak, and there were suddenly lots of other penguins looking at him and laughing as the tape clicked off.

This time it would be different, he was on his own now, and he looked around carefully.

Dave was more of a doing sort of penguin, and when he wasn't doing things he liked to contemplate stuff if he had any spare time, work things out, rather than just meditating or tuning in to whatever was going on 'out there'.

However at the moment he was so stressed he was willing to give anything a go.

He started the tape, and the calming relaxing music started to flow into his ears through the headphones, together with a deep mellow echoed voice telling him to find a good quiet place to relax and to lie down somewhere where he would be alone and uninterrupted.

Dave looked at the cliff edge, the ice falling into the sea, and stopped the tape and looked around. *'mmmm, Tricky'* he thought.

Half an hour later Dave settled himself back against the rocky slope just up from the beach in the most comfortable part of the penguin colony.

There were several young penguins looking at him curiously, and also at the **Do Not Disturb** sign that he now had around his neck. He was also sporting a heavily scratched pair of sunglasses that he had found on the beach. This was to prevent him from seeing distractions.

He didn't have a pillow, as suggested, so he led back on the comfortable rocks and took a deep breath and started the tape again.

The music started and the narrator began in his polished voice; "I want you to imagine…" he said "…that you are on a beach, with the waves in the background, and the gentle sea breeze flowing over your body…"

This guy is good thought Dave. The voice then went on to explain what was going to happen and why, what benefits he would get, how it would help him, and how he would feel, and what he would be capable of at the end, and how much better his life would be.

The man was confident that Dave, at the end, would feel even more relaxed than before he started, which was good.

It all sounded good to Dave. He made a quick check around by opening one eye and gave a glare to the sniggering young penguins, who, following the look, decided to leave him alone.

He closed his eyes and settled down to dutifully follow the instructions.

He was then told not to drive a car, or operate any

machines – which sounded very prudent to Dave.

The narrator went on to explain how he would be better off financially, healthier, happier, confident, smarter, more attractive, and get all the things he wanted.

Dave was fairly happy with what he had, and how he was already, he already had all these things, but he was an open minded penguin, and always open to possibilities, even the possibility of improving perfection.

As instructed, he continued to imagine himself in the same place that he was already, listening to the sounds that he was already hearing; the sea, the whales, the wind and the seagulls - so far it was all pretty simple.

Now, Dave had a very good imagination; he could easily create anything in his mind, as long as it wasn't too big for the space. Like say an elephant, he had made that mistake once, *Oh damn*, he thought, there it was now, large, grey, awkward, and filling all the room in his mind again.

Concentrate he reminded himself. His mind was wandering off again, and he snapped it back to the voice on the tape.

Dave was then told to say and repeat some statements to himself, 'mantas' they were called, like hypnotic rays of hope – or something like that - he repeated the words.....

"Every day, in every way, things are going to be the same as yesterday sound the same as the day before that" Dave said to himself, which was what he thought he was supposed to say.

Dave liked that. He liked things the same, and yesterday had been good, which meant tomorrow would be good too. 'No changes', that was all very 'reassuring', he wiggled his rear end to settle himself down more comfortably in-between the boulders, and then safely relaxed.

He was then told to breathe deeply, in, and out, in and out, several times. Which he did. It made him feel a bit giddy, a bit like brain freeze, when you had eaten too much snow, or eaten the wrong sort of fish, so he slowed the breaths down a bit, and that helped somewhat.

He could never work out why he didn't get brain freeze when the temperature dropped to -50c, but eat even a small bit of snow and *whoosh* there it went again, that numbing pain in the head, unable to think and cursing yourself for being so stupid, again.

Concentrate, he shook his head and listened carefully, trying to not get distracted.

Dave was then asked to count down slowly from ten to one, breathing deeply and slowly each time. This made Dave very tense for a moment, for obvious reasons, until the narrator started counting down for him, and he was able to let out a sigh of relief.

He was then told to imagine himself breathing though his skin, his pores, and imagining that he was his own breath.

That though was a little tricky for Dave; he couldn't imagine how the air was going to make it all the way from his lungs though all those thick layers of rippling muscles. But he gave it a go.

He then had to try and 'see' his breath; imagine and

visualise his breath, which was easy, especially as it was already -30c.

Breathing seemed to be a big part of the tape, important, in-out, in-out, in-out stuff, which was fine until the narrator forgot to mention that he could breathe out at one point, and he nearly died.

He found himself gasping for air, and opened one eye to make sure nobody had seen him, but oddly he was quite alone now. In fact everyone seemed to be keeping a good long safe respectful distance away from him now.

He closed his eyes again, safe in the knowledge that he could relax again in peace. The narrator informed him that any distractions or noises from outside wouldn't disturb him, in fact they would help him relax. Dave doubted this as it seemed like a contradiction, but he decided to wait and see.

He was told that he could manifest anything he wanted, be anything he wanted, he just had to think positively, train his mind, to focus on what he desired, and his mind would ask it of the universal mind and then anything was achievable.

This is great, Dave thought, because he had always wanted to fly, it was his dream, his passion, and first on his bucket list.

Well actually he wanted everyone to fly, he wasn't a selfish penguin, he wanted everyone to be happy, and what was the point of flying if you didn't have anyone else to share it with.

He was then asked to imagine a balloon on the top of his head, like a bubble that he should inflate with all his worries and troubles and stress. With every breath out he should fill the balloon, then let it go, and it would fly away.

Dave tried hard, but he couldn't imagine it inflating at all, the balloon just stayed limp and flopped over to one side. Dave wondered what this meant, but he put it down to the fact that he must already be stress free.

He was then instructed to tense and relax different parts of his body, starting from the top of his head moving down to his feet, which, he was told, would take away the tension and allow the muscles and tendons to relax.

He was successful with his head and feet parts, but identifying the other described body parts in-between was somewhat tricky, everything was a little 'vague' down there, and it was quite hard identifying which muscles were where, if at all – but he did the best he could.

Tense, relax, tense, relax. It seemed to be working, but frankly, it was absolutely exhausting.

There were then lots of other instructions and suggestions, with clicking of fingers, with lots of 'you wills' and 'shalls' and 'going tos', followed by various other set commands. Which of course he followed to the letter, as suggested.

Dave was then asked to imagine himself on top of a very tall crystal skyscraper, this skyscraper was his mind, and he was going to explore it.

He knew what a skyscraper was, but this was a real shock to Dave.

Dave had always thought of his mind as more of a small bungalow, or beach hut, with just a TV, some magazines, a comfy sofa, and a fish freezer in it. Oh and the large hole in one of the walls where he frequently had to chase the elephant out.

This was impressive, a giant building. Dave liked having a big mind; tall, see-through, up in the clouds, higher than the annoying seagulls with stupid names, and high above everyone else. This was amazing, and he suddenly felt very important.

He was told that the tower held all the levels of his mind, and he could travel to anywhere within it, and to places outside of the tower, and to other towers.

He was now at the Beta level of his mind, the fully conscious wide awake top levels, and he would be descending down through Alpha, though Theta, and then into Delta.

He could make the tower higher later on, up to Gamma levels and beyond, if he so desired. Which all sounded 'cool'.

He would be gently guided down through each of the levels exploring various areas, virtual-scapes, and imaginative constructs. He would be learning habits, techniques, developing tools at different levels of the mind to help him, and would learn how to see into the collective spiritual mindscape, and influence things, and that he was in control and could return to being awake at any time.

Really Cool thought Dave again, but he didn't really understand what it all meant.

He was then told to imagine some lift doors in front of him, on the roof of the skyscraper, which opened onto a lift shaft that went down to every level of his mind - all the way down through this very tall skyscraper - this skyscraper that was his mind, this very tall skyscraper here that he was standing on. *Mmmmm* he thought, *things seemed to be repeated a lot, perhaps the tape was also suitable for people who were slightly deaf or forgetful.*

The doors opened; he was told to walk through them, and to turn around and face the open doors, which he obediently did.

Now Dave was a literal sort of guy, he had a very vivid and precise imagination, and he did what he was told. He was always willing to be open to suggestions, and do what he was asked to do, and his imagination was likewise.

However in this particular instance the narrator had neglected to tell Dave to imagine the lift itself, which most people would have taken for granted, but not Dave.

Dave plummeted………..

The sudden shock made Dave physically jump, and he accidently pressed the fast forward button on the tape player under his wing. Down, down, down, the mind shaft he went, like, well, a falling brick really, accompanied by a high pitched whizzing squeaky voice sound in his ears from the tape as it rifled through the lessons and levels.

Dozens of levels that he would have spent weeks practising getting to, entering, and exploring, flashed past in seconds.

Dave wasn't worried though, he thought it was all part of the course, and he looked on with interest, as it all went by, at speed. Images of open doorways full of interesting things strobing past him like rapidly presented flashcards, colours changing as he went.

He was quite calm and he could feel his breathing and mind slow in frequency as he fell. This was all very interesting stuff.

He was now past the Beta levels and past the Alpha levels and onto the Theta levels.

It was surprising what you could see and take in in just a flash or instant vision, like a photo flashed into the brain of each open doorway as it went past straight into his mind. Whistling past, each doorway giving a brief *woofing* sound in the air as it flashed past.

Also, as the walls were like glass, he could also make out things through them that were on the floors around him, and below. He looked down to the next level and he could see and recognise his spiritual helper, just as Dave had imagined him to look like.

It was Dave but as a cross between a famous penguin scientist, the angel Gabriel, and dressed like Gandalf holding a staff with a beard, coming towards him to greet him with a warming knowing smile.

As Dave appeared in the doorway at velocity his guide's expression changed to that of complete horror realising the situation. "Oh Christ!!!" his 'higher self' called, reaching forward to grab Dave as he sped past.

But he was not quick enough, and Dave looked up to see his head disappearing above, with arm stretched downward and shouting out again "Oh…." something begging with 'f' and ending in '…ing' that Dave didn't recognise, and then a long "hell, nooooooo" came the fading cry from above, and wide eyes disappeared into the darkness above.

The last thing Dave heard was his spiritual guide's faint voice calling out in the distance above, "Grab the cables, grab the bloody cables" and then it was gone.

Dave looked around behind him, and sure enough there were a couple of twisted cables or ropes; there one was silver one and one gold, but they were well out of reach, even if he had hands.

He was now passing the Theta levels, or so it said on the signs on the doors to the floors, as they flashed past. Inside the floors there were brilliantly coloured, intensely vibrant, lands of highly elaborate decoration and fauna.

He had seen lots of them in films like the *Wizard of Oz* and *Alice in Wonderland*, and *Charlie and the Chocolate Factory* but whoever had put these together must have been very busy. They all looked so real, vivid and intense. He was very curious to try and see more, explore them, be hypnotised by the never-ending stories, and imaginative constructs, dimensions and alien places.

One level had colourful coral and fish, with mermaids and alien penguins, all of which he had never seen before. There was even a land full of soft white powder that looked very like home and very inviting, with lots of brightly coloured stars and lights in the sky, like diamonds. Very dreamy like the spectrum of colours you got in the sky in the South some nights. But he had never been there.

The levels started to change and became much harsher, extreme, darker, denser, less colourful and yet more intense. He also started to feel very sleepy. He was now starting to pass the Delta levels.

There were warning signs in funny languages written all over them, and symbols. It was all getting quite brutal, hard, less hypnotic, and very much more threatening, and felt dangerous.

He was very tired now, but he couldn't go to sleep – mainly as he didn't have his teddy with him. Which was very lucky for teddy.

His mind started to reduce its frequency of working, and everything slowed, as if he was watching a slow motion film, the scenes where people would hang in the air for several seconds, arms and legs raised, groaning at each other.

He was now seeing lots of things he didn't like - scary, intense, powerful, dramatic things. It was like being inside a whirlwind of thoughts, visions, and sensations, but unprotected, exposed, unshielded. All this would normally be filtered and translated by his unconscious mind in his sleep.

There were lots of things there he hadn't seen before, and couldn't describe, and seemed to come from somewhere else, somewhere dark, dangerous and brutally unrestrained. He tried closing his eyes and tapping his heels together as he had seen in a film, but he forgot that being a penguin he didn't have any heels, and neither did he have his special weekend sparkly red shoes on.

What had at first been very entertaining views, and an interesting journey, were now getting a little unpleasantly uncomfortable, and all far too much to take in to his small conscious mind.

It was very much more feral, and primitive, animalistic but from animals he didn't recognise, and from long ago.

It was getting darker too, and colder; he was a very long way down now.

It certainly took a long time to fall inside a skyscraper, and he wasn't liking where he was going.

His dreams would normally translate and protect him from all this, but not now. He was now reaching terminal velocity, and he was going to hit the bottom.

Dave tried flapping his wings but it was useless, he was no butterfly. It just resulted in him tipping upside down. He looked down but it was just blackness below with the sides of the shaft opening out and disappearing into nothingness.

He was now facing the cables or whatever they were, that had been behind him. In the darkness they had changed, and they now looked dark blue and black, the only colours he could see.

He waved his wings sideways a bit more slowly and he managed to get his feet around them, twisting. He began to spin upside down, and the cables span with him, and wrapped around his feet. Faster and faster he span until he became very dizzy.

Then suddenly the walls vanished completely and he was out, out into some vast dark cavern, but still falling. Just like Gandalf when he fell with the Balrog.

He couldn't see the sides of the cavern but he could feel the vastness of it, the depth.

Down, down, he could see dark water far below him now - black cold, and deep, like you had deep below the big icebergs, far out in the ocean at night. It was swirling around, like giant whirlpools off as far as he could see into the dark.

A giant whirlpool was below him, vast, with smaller whirlpools within it, churning and flowing. He was going to die, he knew that now.

Yet the water was very beautiful though, in its own way - dark, forbidding, vast, cold, yet beautiful. It was like he was inside an unimaginably vast well; a well of penguin souls and minds, with all their memories and knowledge held therein, and he was the bucket.

He felt the cables tighten around his ankles and the soles of his feet. Where the spiralling had become too much for the cables they started to tense and stretch, then they went taut in an elastic reaction slowing his descent. Slowing, slowing.

It was the mother of all bungee jumps, his mates would be so proud.

The water came up fast. He flinched as his head went into the icy water. It was instant and vast. In that split second he knew everything, everything that every penguin had ever known; all the experience, skills, knowledge, understanding and comprehension was there all in his mind, all at once.

It was as if his mind was in some vast swirly flowing field thing, where all information was instantaneous, and there all at the same moment. There was no time here, no distance, no space, yet everything made so much sense.

This was the collective penguin mind consciousness thing he had been told about, but it was not in a form that he could cope with in his own conscious mind. Amazing, he thought.

While he was there, he thought, he would maybe try and influence things, change what was in the mind with his thoughts. It was something to do after all. So he imagined a sea full of fish in the waters where he lived, they were all big and tasty, slow and easy to catch, millions of them.

Worth a try, he thought. But it was somehow exhausting draining all his energy, painful to do, and his mind ached.

He knew he could get the answers to Everything. He thought for a moment, *How do I defeat polar bears?* As he thought, images of polar bears; what they were, what they looked like, everything about them came into his mind.

Then the answer came clearly and precisely to him in his mind, without ambiguity, and it was ….

.. *Don't be so bloody stupid…*

… then it all stopped.

He was being pulled out of the water fast, flying back up, out, out of the cavern, and up, up, up into the shaft again.

Someone was pulling him up, he looked up again past his feet, and there was light, light coming from above at the end of the tunnel above.

It looked so attractive, welcoming, warm, away from the cold depths he had been in, something was pulling him out. *Probably Gandalf* he thought.

Then it all vanished. It was dark, and he woke up. He opened his eyes, sat up, and he realised now that he was back on the beach again.

But everyone had gone, vanished, the sky looked different, and so did the snow and ice.

He still felt upside down.

There was a growl from behind him. He turned in horror to see a massive white four-legged polar bear with massive teeth snarling at him several feet away; it had long claws and a hungry look, and he could smell it's breath.

Dave's stomach turned, which was quite a significant manoeuvre. Fear took him and he froze, he closed his eyes as he could not face the thought of seeing his own death, and this was as near death as he had ever come.

Then there was a loud click.

The tape had stopped, and the **Play** button had popped back up on his tape recorder.

Then he REALLY woke up this time.

Dave slowly opened his eyes, and looked up to a sky that he recognised, and sounds around him of other penguins.

His body felt like heavy rocks, everything was brightly coloured and vivid and intense around him, he looked around all the other penguins on the beach and they all looked very strange, sort of glowing.

But they were also all very excited about something, and they all seemed to be preparing to go off somewhere, somewhere out to sea.

Dave wondered what the fuss might be all about.

It had all been a bit much for Dave, a crash course into the depths of the mind and into everyone else's.

Down all the way to the bottom without stopping, and yet having a clear picture of what was going on without being hypnotically drawn in to the other levels on the way.

Mistakes happen in life - that's how we learn, evolve and change. But then again sometimes things aren't mistakes, and it was surprising what things you could find on a beach that weren't necessarily there by coincidence.

Dave didn't just throw the tape away, that wouldn't be very ecologically friendly, he just put it in the bottom of his rucksack, and got out his Meatloaf tape again.

He stood up, and waddled back to his patch to look after the egg again, resembling in the twilight, a somewhat pedestrianized and slightly overweight *Bat Out of Hell.*

If you were kind…. and squinted a lot.

4 SOMETHING FLUFFY THIS WAY COMES

It was six o'clock in the morning and Dave was just in the middle of a dream.

He had programmed his mind to set an alarm off in his head, and it had gone off as it was supposed to, bang on time.

Dave had never worked out how it did that, it was a real mystery. Especially as his higher self or his consciousness thing knew less about clocks than he did.

However, when asking his 'spiritual guide' to set his mental wake up alarm for the morning, he had neglected to specify the day of the week, and consequently a whole week had gone missing, somewhere.

Dave hadn't slept at all well through with all that sunshine, and his dreams had been vivid and dramatic and memorable. Which was always an indication that something was going on somewhere, and not just in his head.

He opened an eye wearily, and looked forward, which was usually the easiest direction.

Standing a few feet in front of him was a large ball of grey fluff, with a beak, feet, and two black expectant eyes looking straight at him.

It was jigging from side to side in a keen sort of 'motivational' manner…. Dave just looked at it, blankly.

It was also at that point that Dave was surprised at

how cold and draughty his feet felt. It was one of those hypnogogic disoriented moments, where you were trying to make sense of a situation, and get a perceiving grasp on a reality.

A stark harsh unprepared reality feeling, that you had been thrown too many large spanners at once.

He tried the 'closing the eyes and opening them and blinking again', thing.

It didn't work, it was still there, jigging and beaming.

His brain was trying to form coherence in a logical progressive lateral manner, and started off on the *was it male or female* thing, with the first of the 20 questions. Was it a girl penguin thing or a boy penguin thing? Somehow he couldn't think of the gender collective name for penguins.

Why couldn't he think of it, what was the term ?

He had to somehow come up with the right gender name, bring it to mind, or the thing in front of him couldn't be given a name, and subsequently it wouldn't exist.

So, for the moment, he decided to call the thing 'IT' - just to be safe. IT was still there. Dave squinted, but it still didn't help.

Everything was still all too much, so he closed his eyes again, just to rest for a moment, just for a five more minutes, just ease himself back gently into the dream he was in before.

His dream had been nice soft and fluffy, welcoming, and he mentally went to wrap himself back up in his quilt, and press the **Snooze** button on the bedside table in his mind.

He pressed it – but the button wasn't the same, somehow it had changed, now it had the 'F' word on it, in big flashing illuminated letters. Which then set off a different alarm, a sort of panic alarm, and all sorts of things happened at once.

His body and brain kicked in the door of his mind's bedroom. His eyes opened wide, adrenaline flowing. His heart raced, and he stood bolt upright, breathing hard, and stared at the now grinning face in front of him.

"Hello Dad!" IT said.

Dave was doing the maths in rapid jerky equations.

A few moments later, Dave gave a tentative nervous wave, and smiled, awkwardly.

IT waved back. Dave looked left, and then right for more reality. But there were no more handles with which to grab.

A moment later, Dave's wife arrived with some fish in her beak, and without looking at Dave she bent forward and posted the fish into the now open mouth of …… IT.

This had clearly been going on for some time. Surprisingly though, she didn't give Dave any of the 'you useless father' looks that he was expecting, she just looked at him and smiled and whispered something to the… to the… chick, which giggled, and then she wandered off again.

Over the next few weeks he would be let off fatherly duties altogether, which in the state he was in was just as well.

He tried, but thankfully it was a good thing they had chick nurseries these days, where all the chicks could be grouped together in the middle of the colony, safe and protected, and away from harm, and useless fathers like him.

Dave couldn't see why they couldn't do things the way the turtles did, what was wrong with just dumping the eggs on a beach covering them over and legging it? Then there was no responsibility, no having to look back, and no school fees.

Mind you turtles were very stupid creatures; perhaps there was something in the nurturing process, or something to do with warm sand rather than the only option here which was snow. What was wrong with the concept of sink or swim? All the turtles he knew were good at both.

However, penguins thought that bringing up their young properly was a very responsible thing, and everyone was very clear about what had to be done and how to do it.

Dave just wished he was better at it, and had more energy, and that he didn't feel so guilty.

He remembered seeing with everyone else a natural history documentary with a Rockhopper penguin in it that had adopted a group of stray Emperor penguin chicks.

It had, surprisingly, protected them from an evil Petrel, and had then gathered them together. However it then started herding them, pushing and encouraging the chicks, onward, and over to the edge of the ice into the sea.

There had been gasps. It was obvious to Dave, and all the other penguins watching the documentary, that the chicks couldn't swim, they hadn't grown their waterproof feathers yet, and they would drown with their soft fluffy ones.

Young emperor penguins should never be made to go into the purifying water, and should always be allowed to make their own choice of jumping in, if they wanted to, when they were older and ready.

This didn't happen with Rockhoppers, they were pushed in to the water from an early age, but this wasn't this Rockhoppers flock, and the same rules didn't apply. Instead of leading them to safety, he was leading them to be drowned, through blind ignorance.

There were screams of fury directed at the screen.

Luckily the chicks had all survived but there was still outrage, and it nearly caused a war.

If their colony had been any closer, and not the other side of the sea lions, there probably would have been one.

The Rockhopper was probably just doing what it thought was right, protecting the chicks and getting them into the water, but that was always the risk when you did things that you thought were obvious, when you didn't understand what you were doing…

.. The implications could be catastrophic.

There was certainly too much of that going on in the world.

Luckily IT's mother seemed to know what to do, and it wouldn't be long before the swimming lessons would start, and IT would be away, and he wouldn't feel so guilty any more..

5 DAVE HEADS SOUTH

It had been a very foggy morning, but frankly that wasn't really much of an excuse.

Dave had woken up early and had set off towards the sea to do some fishing, or at least that's where he thought he was going. It seemed like a good idea to get an early 'fish in', while they were still waking up, and before everyone else got there.

It was only about an hour later, wandering through the fog, that he started to think that the sea was, well, much further away than he remembered. But with his unfailing sense of direction he knew he was going the right way, so he carried on.

One foot after the other, on and on he walked.

After a while he just relaxed, knowing he would be there at some point, eventually.

It was all OK, besides he could use the time to think, contemplate, relax, and just chill, and lose any track of time. It was fairly easy really, there being no night-time here in the summer. He just left his penguin body device in 'homing' autopilot, and carried on walking.

He had his shades on and was listening to his Genesis albums through his headphones.

Three weeks later Dave's feet were starting to ache a bit, so he stopped.

Sweat was also starting to drip down his forehead in the heat, so he removed his sunshades to wipe his face. It was at that point that he realised that it wasn't foggy at all. His glasses were the only things fogged up - aside from his brain - and had misted up from all the dried sea spray.

Easy mistake to make, he thought.

Bright sunshine shone out on the open snow plain, and he realised that he was in the middle of nowhere. He started to panic now. He had no idea where he was. All he knew was that he had been going completely in the wrong direction, away from the sea rather than towards it, South rather than North.

THIS WAS BAD!

He swallowed hard. He was lost, a long way from home, and on his own, and the batteries had run out on his tape player. Not good for a penguin.

He took a moment to calm down and looked around; there was nothing, not even a mirage to lead him astray. It was just white and flat, in every direction.

After about ten minutes of patiently standing hoping the problem would go away, he noticed a flash in the distance, a brief reflection from something, just for an instant.

With no other options open to him, he headed off in the direction of the flash.

An hour later a strange structure came into view.

It was a collection of giant silver and grey half-buried tin cans. They had long twigs poking out from them into the air and long bits of wire attached. There were also lots of parallel line tracks in the snow all around them. The tracks appeared to have been made by a jet ski, specifically a ski-doo MXZ model, but he couldn't be absolutely sure at this range.

There was also a very large stick with wires on it some way away that was dozens of times higher than Dave, and they seemed to be giving off a buzzing noise that made his head feel funny, spinny, like he didn't know where he was.

He didn't like it.

As he got closer he could see the tracks went off towards some larger, square, brown and white shaped objects further on, and also to a big silver dome thing, as if the moon had fallen into the snow. There were also lots of brightly coloured national flags flying, which Dave deduced, had obviously been stolen from ships.

There was also a silver ball thing on a post, with red and white eels spiralling around the post.

Dave decided he needed a closer look. It was very quiet so he guessed everyone must be off fishing.

He carefully waddled up to the nearest giant tin thing, stretched up on his toes, and looked inside through one of the square clear ice things on the side.

The inside was very complicated; there were lots of things that he didn't recognise, lots of shapes he didn't understand, so he couldn't see them in his mind, as they didn't make sense to him.

In one area, on a sheet of flat wood, raised up high, there were some penguins in a clear ice box with a headlamp above them. There were two Chinstrap penguins and a Rockhopper. Dave didn't like Rockhoppers, they were aggressive and rude.

One had shouted at him once and made a rude gesture at him, which he had never forgotten, so from then on he made a point of leaving them alone.

Dave was going to wait until it saw him, and then he was going to get the rude gesture in first. But it looked like it was asleep.

Lucky for him thought Dave, and then he felt a bit guilty, and a bit sad for it.

The whole area inside seemed to be full of biological things; green things, like seaweed, but growing upwards. Fish and whales that he recognised were there, but flat, and on the wall. It seemed a strange place to be trying to keep, look at, and grow living things in.

Dave waddled around to the front of the hut and looked for a way in to see if there was anyone who could help.

He knocked on the door with his beak and waited. There was no reply, but he could hear a lot of laughter coming from inside. They seemed to be coming closer to the door so he politely stepped back.

Suddenly the door burst open and several people emerged carrying buckets of ice water. Dave was anxious at first and wandered what he had done to offend them.

He stepped to the side but they seemed not to have noticed him at all, they were far too interested in themselves, talking and laughing. Two of the men had no clothes on their top halves.

The two men then proceeded to kneel down, and were handed the buckets of ice water. They then poured the water over their heads, screamed, and everyone laughed, and took photos.

Then they all ran back inside quickly, straight past Dave, leaving him with his wing still raised, poised to ask a question. The door slammed closed.

Dave stood there motionless, his beak wide open.

Humans were very odd things, they seemed quite reasonable, responsible, mature and 'OK' individually, but when they got into a group they started to behave quite differently, childish, immature, mad, and it got worse the larger the group got. This group seemed to be behaving like a young teenager, doing stupid mindless things.

Yet the group operated in slow time compared to how an individual would act and respond, oblivious to responsibility and the surroundings, and then dashing back inside to its gadgets.

What, thought Dave, *would they be like if there were thousands of them?* Dave shuddered at the thought - *a baby? Plants in a greenhouse?*

After several moments of trying to get some sort of hold on reality, another question came into his mind. *How had they not seen him?* It was as if he was invisible. It was as if he were a ghost.

These were very strange people, and he was now unsure if he actually wanted their help now.

Dave looked sideways. To his right there was a round cage; it was about the same height as him, with a lid on it and it had a black plastic bag inside.

Dave was wary of black bags; he had heard a lot of stories about penguins being taken away in them. But this one smelt very interesting, a sort of 'foody' sort of smell.

He carefully waddled over to it and stuck his head under the lid. It smelt good inside. He tried to climb up the side of the cage to get in but it toppled backwards and he fell in as it fell over. In so doing so hit his head on the lid, and passed out.

He woke up with his head in a newspaper, he pulled himself back out of the waste bin, and the newspaper came out with him. He looked down at it sprawled in front of him. He read the writing on the front. It was named '*The Sun*'.

He read the front page, which seemed to be a list of problems and things to get you worried about, arguments, and important things that were going on in the world with famous people's personal problems. He turned it over and on the back there were more people fighting, in teams, in reds and blues, and their personal problems too, and people called 'fans' who also fought each other.

Knowledge kept coming into Dave's head from some collective place, about what it all meant, what was going on, on lots of different levels. Dave hadn't even realised he could now read. It all made sense, but only in one way. He flipped the paper over again, and turned to the third page.

These people were clearly also very interested in biology.

He tried to process what he was seeing. The words at the top said 'Hot Chick'. Below them was a naked human female, not a bird at all, and she was about to eat a long piece of coloured ice on a stick.

She didn't look hot at all - even Dave could tell that she was obviously very cold.

His head was starting to ache a bit now from all the information coming in. He flicked through the other pages reading the articles on politics, and who was saying what about what other people had said on what shows. Information on what people had done wrong, and where they may be on holiday now. What countries were saying what about each other, and why they were sending their people to visit others in things called tanks.

It all seemed very negative, there didn't seem to be anything nice or happy or positive at all.

Then he arrived at the crossword page. Dave liked puzzles.

His mind was working so fast now that he could pull in all sorts of knowledge. He looked at the first few questions, and the answers came to him. They seemed remarkably easy, even for a penguin.

The first answer he saw was the word 'Band' – the clue was "As in, Big, should be, and lastic" the second answer was "Width" which was the answer to "What you have when you eat fast food".

He looked at the half filled-in box of squares, and his mind started to play tricks on him; it was filling in the words for him and connecting them in different ways and meanings. BandWidth, Problem, Biological, Data, Field, Genetic, Conflict, Transfer, DNA, Broadband, and *Twin Peaks.*

It was almost as if he were trying to tell himself something, opening his mind - everything suddenly becoming obvious, clear from the connection.

His head really hurt now though, his face felt cold and there was a point in the middle of his head that felt like he had brain freeze from eating snow. It was at one single point in his head.

The top of his skull ached in one spot too, like

someone was continually pouring ice water down onto it in the centre, or there was a cold iron bar, point down, resting on it.

He was processing too much, too fast for his brain; there was too much information coming in and out, linking things together in his mind. It was all too much for his mind to deal with in one go. Worryingly, the something that was giving him all this information that he wanted, didn't seem to realise that.

Like the men with their buckets of iced water, it was too much all at once to cope with. He only had so much BandWidth.

He looked down at the page again, he had solved all the clues now, all but the last one, which was 'Old big ship wot sank'.

Images and thoughts and connections were all firing in his head at once. His mind was working so hard now that his brain started doing strange things. He flicked back through the pages to the front again, images and words leaping out at him; it all made so much sense, but in a mad muddled sort of way.

He could see what was going wrong, he could see and understand everything, overlapping combined thoughts flowing through his head. He made it back to Page 3, his eyes and mind darting from one thing to another, '*Titanic*' went through his mind.

He felt giddy and fell forwards face down into the newspaper. Before he lost consciousness the last things to come into his mind were a couple of icebergs.

He woke up still face down, groaning, feeling exhausted and awful. There were lots of flashing lights going on around him, there were also lots of people taking pictures and videos of him.

He was then placed carefully onto an open net, which ironically was also where most of the photos and videos would end up in a few hours, and then 'go viral' a few hours after that.

Dave was going to be famous, but not in a good way.

They put him in a box, then on a plane and they took him back to where he had come from.

A few days later, all the excitement had died down, and he was settled back in the colony again, on his home patch.

For days, he tried to explain what he had seen to the rest of the penguins. He tried to describe the 'home of the jet ski people', and the 'inside' places where they lived, everything.

But the penguins couldn't see what he was trying to describe, they couldn't visualise it all, they had no point of reference. He had nothing to describe it to in relation to, or with anything they knew of.

He tried drawing pictures in the snow, but he wasn't very good at drawing, and they didn't seem to mean anything to any of them.

Eventually even the ones that believed him just wandered off, it was almost as if the whole idea had gone from their heads, been moved out for some reason, replaced by more interesting things.

He just couldn't get through to them, or make them see, or perhaps they didn't care.

Until they themselves had seen it, perceived it, understood, then it all meant nothing.

As far as they were concerned it was all in Dave's mind, all in his dreams, and it didn't affect them so why did they care.

But Dave knew different.

It seemed very odd to Dave, why it all just didn't mean anything to them.

They had their view of the world, and what was in it, and that was that. It was the way that some penguins just didn't even want to know, they had their own lives and weren't even interested.

Unless it directly affected them or threatened or benefited them, they didn't care.

Some couldn't believe it all or didn't allow themselves to, or were prevented from doing so, by what they had been told to believe already. Yet some did believe him but just got on with things anyway and then forgot. It was a strange situation, it didn't make much sense to Dave.

He wanted to get them to go south with him and see. To follow his trail and see what he saw, and then they would understand, believe him and make sense of what he was trying to explain to them, and then they could do something about it.

But nobody was interested, nobody seemed to care that much, it wasn't their problem, and they didn't need to know.

They thought they were fine as they were, but Dave knew different.

His brain device was still processing things for his mind, and it still ached, but it seemed to be going over old ground now, looping through the same concepts and ideas, but without the same immediate 'in the now' productive flowing two-way energy.

However when he closed his eyes he could immediately see a big black sign in front of him in the dark, a few feet in front of his face. It was in high definition and widescreen with white letters on it, it said

'EMPTY THE ATTIC'.

Dave didn't know what an attic was but he understood what it meant, or was trying to say.

He had to be more careful of himself, and his brain, and how he was using it.

Like his body, his brain could only do so much, and he had to get it into habits, be organised with his thoughts, interpret what was coming in, what he thought about, focused on, and manage his mind and what it was doing.

He remembered one of those management audio tapes he had heard some months ago, about having SMART objectives, that was it.

He had to have…

Specific **M**anageable **A**chievable **R**ealistic and **T**ime bounded jobs to do in his head.

Unfortunately the collective mind thing had no clue whatsoever about SMART objectives, at all, or even data bandwidth, or even what a penguin was for that matter.

Which was a little worrying.

Especially if you were dealing with things and thoughts 'in the now', live processing as it were, trying at the same time to work out the context of what it was trying to get across, what the hell it was on about, and work out what needed to happen.

All at the same time.

Yet more importantly - WHY HIM??

It didn't seem to have his interests and needs at heart - only its own. It didn't seem to care much for him either, only so far as his mind was working, a bit like a slave.

He put his cleaned shades on, and his headphones, and waddled off towards the sea - in the right direction this time.

He was going to tsunami and jet-spray out his mental attic, sun bleach his brain, clear his head, empty his mind, and do a bit of surfing and fishing to get himself fit at the same time.

It was a bloke thing..

Dave wasn't a religious penguin.

In fact he didn't believe in the penguin 'god' at all, or at least in any penguin 'god' that religions seem to try to describe or define.

To Dave they all just didn't make sense, add up, or equate and stand up to any form of logic at all.

Of course not having any evidence or a detailed explanation of what 'god' actually was came as a bit of a stumbling block for penguin religions as well.

As did all the bad and unjust things that went on in the real world that 'god' was supposed to be in charge of, or looking after; things that all appeared to be getting worse, not better.

There weren't any logical explanations from religions as to why it was all going so badly wrong, and why it was all frankly a bit rubbish, compared to how it used to be.

Dave had done quite a bit of reading on the subject of religion, in books, and on the Internet, and like most intellectually structured created thinking forms, they always seemed to end up with the problem of the 'elephant in the room' again.

That elephant of course, as in physics, was that uncomfortably large awkward problem that wouldn't go away.

One that required some sort of faith, a leap of logic, or a mental bridge, for the large gap in the plausibility to work, when you clearly couldn't join up all the dots, as half the numbers you had been given were missing.

Dave had also studied philosophy, psychology, physics, and a couple of other things beginning with 'p', and they all ended up not being able to come up with a big answer, the final solution, the ultimate picture. That of what was really there, what it all meant, who was in charge, what was for, and why we existed.

Which should all be fairly simple really, and probably not 42.

Even music, which had a set language and had evolved over time, seemed to be inspired from somewhere else, but music didn't have the answers either. But it was nice.

The same was true with a lot of art. Even though the best art was unstructured, untethered and inspired by 'something higher' - it still seemed to just end up with not saying anything, evolving into something more and more surreal, using virtual concepts, and non-located expressions over time.

Even the artists themselves were turning into faceless hermits, ending up producing vapourware placed in remote empty spaces. They were all desperately trying to 'articulate' something that they had experienced, something 'not real' that they wanted to describe somehow; put the formless into form, which in itself was also evolving.

The same could also be said about architecture, or fashion in general, which was mostly driven by the mind of the consumer, and in turn was influenced by the changing collective taste.

Fashion wasn't really Dave's thing, it just seemed a bit, well, 'girlie', but he did like things to look nice, whatever that was.

Dave had read in various penguin religious literature, and on the Internet, that long, long ago, the Penguin God had been a great giant seal. He was vindictive, frightening, and ate bad penguins.

In other later articles the god was a polar bear, which had lots of different interpretations and forms, as nobody knew what they actually looked like or were.

This had caused lots of fights long ago in the ancient past, with the need to make sacrifices to it to make it feel better about itself, and to fend off bad storms.

Curiously the shape and nature of the Penguin God always changed into the form defined by whoever won the fights.

Then, over time, it had changed to become multiple penguin gods all existing at the same time. They all did different things, and had different personalities and roles.

They also had different feelings, and represented lots of ideas, and far away things. However they all knew what they were doing and had a hierarchy. There were male and female ones too, and they were all there to do different special 'jobs'. But they didn't seem to have much of a clue about real people, and used the World as a sort of board game.

Which sounded exciting and made good stories that Dave liked to read about and watch in films.

Years later, after many more fights, it had all

changed again, and the god had become just one giant penguin that lived on top of the highest mountain on a throne made of pure, smooth, shiny nesting stones.

There had even been a lot of fights about what colour the stones were, and what the Penguin God had said and revealed. There were also lots of numbers and symbols used, and promises of things being better, and a sense of urgency.

It was eventually agreed that there were lots of different coloured stones, and that there were fifty different shades of them between white and black.

Then some time ago, some hero penguin named 'Dave' had climbed the mountain to say 'Hello', and found that their god wasn't there at all.

God had obviously moved, and had even taken the throne and the stones too.

Now it was an all-seeing, all-knowing, almighty penguin god, who lived up high in the clouds. However, Dave knew quite a bit about clouds, and their capacity for supporting large penguins and thrones, and he also knew about the painful nature of gravity.

He had tried to explain these fundamental scientific and practical problems to some of the penguin clan elders, and had been confronted with a hail of abuse and ridicule, along with a few small stones.

He was also about to ask the obvious question that nobody else seems to have thought to ask - the "Yes - but what is it?" one, but after the initial response, he thought better of it.

Clearly these were special magic clouds, and he should not question the existence or the nature of the great Penguin God.

The situation was a bit like one of his favourite Monty Python films, but in this instance it didn't seem very funny.

What really confused Dave though, was the fact that no one had ever mentioned that they were magic clouds, or explained how they worked.

It then struck him that there was somewhat of an evolutionary pattern forming here, which was also in line with a lot of the evolution of all the other areas he had studied, especially Biology. Something of a trend.

He also asked what had happened to all the other gods - the ones that they had been so sure were there long ago - and asked why they had changed. He had also explained to the elders that it was all a never ending self-adapting belief and control structure for the scientifically unexplainable, a childish protective mental bubble developed in the unconscious psyche. One which still made no logical sense.

Then he was really told off….. very loudly.

They didn't agree with him. Obviously whatever it was, wasn't that keen to evolve or change, and had quite a strong resistance to nosey smartarse penguins.

So he went off and trawled through his collection of 1980's video documentaries, and behind his mint condition set of David Attenborough ones, he found a set called *The Day the Universe Changed*. They had been made in 1985 and were written and presented by James Burke, but Dave realised that he had never seen them, which was curious as he liked the previous 'connections' ones, and he loved *Tomorrow's World*, with all those strange *Space 1999* ideas.

He loved the ones where it showed how we would all be going to go around in cars that flew, that the world would be one big computer, and that we would get machines to do everything, and how everyone would look like they were having a nice happy time and be permanently on holiday.

Later, having watched them all, Dave came up with many new ideas and started to show the other penguins all the films. He wrote down his thoughts, and drew some artistic pictures (because only some of the penguins could read).

Dave was all fired up now, just like Moses was when he came down from the mountain with his tablets - which must have been pretty good ones.

Dave had been energised and began talking inspirationally about what he has seen and how it was all true, and tried to get everyone to see and understand, and most importantly, to change.

Quite a number of the penguins did like the stuff he was talking about and showing them, but the majority just seemed to be more stimulated by his charismatic energy.

They seemed to gravitate towards him, and be attracted to his interesting magnetic personality. They were happy to go along with it, watch, and be drawn along by the exciting ambiance being generated by the rest of the crowd.

It's what everyone else was doing after all.

So things finally seemed to be going very well for Dave, and he presented more and more information and ideas, and he became more and more self-stimulated.

He had quite a bit of a momentum going.

The trouble began because of the very last thing he said, which was just before the crowd turned on him. It went something like, "This wonderful human being has shown us the way forward and we should all follow him", and there were even cheers from the crowd, "From this day forward I say we should all call ourselves….. 'Burkes'…"

… And that's where it all very quickly started to go very rapidly downhill…

Then a week later he was standing alone at the base of the mountain, far away from the main group, covered in bruises and sticky plasters.

Now and then one of the penguins would come past and shout something like "Idiot" or throw a snowball at him.

It wasn't a good time for Dave…...

In Reality, thought Dave, *penguins just want to hear what they want to hear*. It was hard to get penguins that had been beguiled and hypnotised to believe in something else, to see or understand things from another perspective. It took a lot of energy to get them to change their minds.

It was too easy, as he had just found out, to fall into the same trap that others had done. Those that had tried to make penguins understand, to wake up.

It just wasn't enough to *know*, you had to be able to explain it in a progressive way, to allow penguins to go from one state to another in easy steps, without rocking the boat.

Equally, if you *were* ever to find someone who really knew what was going on and who had proof of it, then due to the collective nature of it all, it was likely that nobody would be allowed to see, hear, or read what they had written anyway.

Even if they were able to understand it. You also had to step back and ask why this was happening and why what they knew was being deliberately hidden away? As if something was hiding itself in a self-adapting controlling way, and always one step ahead of common knowledge.

It was a tricky problem.

Then two weeks later everything changed again.

The elders met and brought all of the penguins together, in a bunch.

There were hundreds of them; all packed tightly en masse, all looking up at the elders who stood on a small snow mound that they, supposedly, had made.

The high elder came forward carrying his sacred driftwood staff; it had a skull on the top and the name of their god on the back, which everyone knew was 'Skelator'.

The penguin elder spoke in a deep, assertive voice. He told them that, apparently, the Penguin God had moved again, and that his new home had been revealed to one of them in a vision one night. God was now in some invisible dimension, and he had given a long list of more revelations.

The elder read through the list, and the Penguin God seemed to be using the same sort of words and ancient way of speaking as he had used when he spoke on top of the mountain. He had also become angry with those that had questioned his existence and his nature.

Anyone so doing so in the future, he continued, would spend all of eternity in the deep, dark penguin volcanic lava toilet cave under the ground…

There were gasps.

Everyone knew about the fiery toilet cave. Everyone…

Then, slowly, they all turned and looked straight at Dave.

Dave took a step backwards into the space that was now clearing all around him, and suddenly the bruises on his body were the last thing on his mind.

Now Dave was good at thinking on his feet, which considering he rarely, if ever, laid down, was just as well. He recognised the somewhat frosty glares, the uncompromising ignorance, the collective resistance to change of several hundred penguins all of one mind. He also noted the multitude of rocks and stones around, and decided to 'take the initiative'.

"I will," said Dave tentatively "Venture forth and find this invisible dimension and humbly apologise to the almighty Elephant Penguin God, and beg his forgiveness, and I shall not return until I do."

That got them….

Dave could sense the logic gears churning in the minds of the penguins, trying to work out if he was politically outsmarting them, if he was genuine, or in fact for the most part – what the bloody hell he was going on about.

What else could he do? They weren't being allowed to see things from his perspective, they couldn't or didn't want to come out of their programmed comfy quilt bubbles of belief and control. They could not see things from his viewpoint, it was too 'difficult', too 'unprotected', and they were much happier being safely inside their protected hypnotised terra firma perceptive couch potato worlds.

Change, after all, was always difficult, especially when you didn't know any different, when it wasn't necessary, when you couldn't see anything wrong, and when you were programmed to do set things.

Yet before they had even got onto the metaphysical discussions with reference to the elephant, Dave had already decided not to wait around.

He didn't wait for the interrupt protocols, the logic circuits of the mental control and belief structures to resolve themselves and invoke action, along with the accompanying rocks and pitchforks. He simply headed in the direction of the hills in the distance at quite some speed; at a rate that was impressive even for him.

He was in an even worse place now. After several hours of waddling he reached the base of one of the smaller hills that formed part of the foothills of the largest mountain in the area.

He didn't have a clue why he had walked that way; it was just big, and there, and something to head for, away from trouble.

Now his feet hurt and he was tired and hungry, and he was breathing hard.

He stopped to catch his breath; he felt quite giddy. It was surprisingly beautiful here, quiet, unspoiled, pristine. The giant rocky snow- covered mountain above him was mirrored in the ice sheet before him.

It looked just like two mountains, one the upside

down mirror image of the other. It was so clear and bright and sharp that it was almost impossible to tell which mountain was real and which was the reflected image.

It was then that he saw a pure powder-white arctic hare (which was very strange considering where he was). It ran straight towards him and then dashed past him, almost as if he wasn't there, and then disappeared down into a hole in the side of the mountain and vanished.

Curious thought Dave.

Now Dave was sensible, and he knew that what he was seeing wasn't real, but as he hadn't taken any recreational drugs or hit his head, he needed to know what it was all about.

Without thinking first, he went into the entrance of the hole and fell in, and then down, down, down, just as expected.

Down, down and more down the tunnel he went, *Which is quite logical,* thought Dave, as he fell.

Even though he knew it was imaginary he still kept his wings and feet tucked in; it was always hard to get out of habits, and the hypnotic effect of illusions.

Still, there's no harm in that, always better to err on the safe side, you know, just in case it turns out to be real, even if it is a different sort of 'real', he thought

Then logic went out the window as he emerged with a **thump** on the floor of a very large, white, well lit square room.

There were stairs going down to a basement, and lots of strange things all around him, including a brightly coloured chandelier swinging from the ceiling.

This is all in your mind Dave told himself. Which was quite a big thing for him to realise.

Dave had also worked out the truth in his mind; it wasn't a great penguin in the sky after all, it was just an elephant.

It was now looking at him from the other side of the room. It was really there - he could see it out of the corner of his eye - in the corner of this large room; there, large, awkward, and big.

It had an embarrassed, guilty look, suddenly realising for itself what it was, and expecting him to sort the problem out.

To resolve the awful chaos in this 'Haven' place in which it stood. Dave knew it was called that, as there was a sign above the entrance where he fell in.

The sign had the word 'Haven' on it with a symbol of a penguin next to it in crayon. Symbols seemed to be important here, it made things simple, like links or connections, just as you had on your desktop.

Dave wondered if there were rooms like this with other symbols on them for other things, like fish, snakes, or stars, to indicate what was in the room, and what you would learn there.

This room clearly did not have any form of en-suite facilities though, and Dave had no intention of even taking a quick look into the basement, as he had a fairly clear idea of what was down there - and it wasn't good.

"Alright Dave?" asked the elephant enthusiastically, and nodded to him in a friendly manner.

Dave ignored it, in the hope that it would just go away.

The elephant in Dave's mind wasn't really an elephant though; again it was just a manifestation of the difficult problem, the unresolved paradigm of what this all was.

It was that awkward issue of something that couldn't be explained away by anything that you knew or understood; that awkward thing that plagued all philosophy, psychology, quantum physics, art, religion and everything else.

It was that 'hang on a minute that doesn't make any logical rational sense' elephant, that you couldn't translate into physical logic, and get your mind around.

Dave knew what the answer was really, you had to have been 'in it' to understand 'it', but he didn't have any way of describing 'it' in any physical or real terminology either, as it wasn't 'like' anything.

Yet everything he knew and perceived had come from it, not the other way around. So the problem remained an elephant for now, and the only way of getting close to defining it or describing it was still through various analogies and descriptive stories.

Dave just carried on ignoring the elephant, and pretended that it wasn't there; just in the same way as everyone else did.

Besides it would be very embarrassing getting caught talking to an imaginary virtual elephant, especially as he didn't even know its name.

Dave did know however that he wasn't going mad.

This was all just here to show something to him, to explain something to himself.

They had said that his late aunt Mildred was mad;

madder than a box of squirrels, apparently. She heard 'voices' all the time, and she thought she was a reincarnation of a flying dolphin called Flipper.

Which was fine, except that of course everyone knew that dolphins didn't come back as penguins, not even ones from TV programmes.

So everyone thought she was mad, all except young Dave; after all she did seem to be the only one in the family that had been happy, and the only one that had interesting conversations with him. He thought that she just had different ways of seeing things.

Things then began changing in the room; objects were being added, like in a progressive dream.

Dave looked up. There was a large clock on the wall. The clock had two sets of hands on it; one set was going forwards and the other was going backwards.

Every time you looked at it, the hands were not in the same place. The clock was clearly useless here and didn't seem to have any purpose other than to explain something; obviously that time was irrelevant here, that it was timeless, a state machine.

He wondered why it didn't just have a sign saying that, instead of some cryptic animated symbol, or perhaps it was unaware of the fact itself.

But then that is why you get representations like this in all those books, films, art and in your dreams; it was trying to represent something in some way that was understandable to you, giving you a story to convey parts of the whole picture.

Curiouser and curiouser thought Dave.

Dave thought he would try something.

"What is the point of that?" he asked of the elephant, and he pointed to the clock "It is totally useless."

"Well," said the elephant "time doesn't exist here. It is meaningless. This is a state environment, and not defined by time. Things here just are, or are not. There is no concept of 'was' or 'will be', other than that which is projected by probability or remembered in memory, in which case they are known and perceived into reality.

"Things just have an informational state, but with projected future probabilities of other states. Yet it knows 'what was', and 'what is' and 'what probably will be', and 'what will be' changes the 'what is' and the 'what was' and vice versa. So you see it's meaningless."

Dave was now wishing he hadn't asked, and he watched the clock intently and without blinking; the hands moved in a gentle flowing motion.

"But when I look at it, it doesn't jump around" said Dave.

"That's because you are giving it meaning by perceiving it; both time and the clock itself. That's what you are here for - to create meaning from the meaningless; to organise stuff along a set of rules and guideline; to evolve" said the elephant.

"It still looks a bit weird if you ask me" said Dave.

"Well yes," said the elephant, who was now wearing a little blue and white dress, "but then everything has errors - nothing is perfect - you just have to try and make sense of things even though they are senseless."

That seems logical, thought Dave. He had no idea why the elephant was wearing the dress now though, but he was a broad-minded and polite penguin, so he didn't ask.

There was now a full length mirror on the wall. Dave went up to it and looked at himself in it.

It showed you everything that you wanted to see, and in the way you thought you wanted to see it. It was a reflection of perceived reality.

Dave was pleased to see that he looked just the same in it as he always did, his mental, or 'higher', 'spiritual' program blueprint looked good, although his six-pack had lost some of its usual toned definition.

He turned sideways-on to check over his profile, and flexed his biceps.

Then suddenly the room changed around him. It was as if he could create any environment he wanted just by thinking about it, imagining it.

His imagination expanded and he could envisage even sharing common game-type holograms with other penguins' minds in other rooms that they might be in. But the change made him tired, it seemed to take some energy from him.

There seemed to be a purpose with us being physical too, being a physical penguin, to see it, experience it, change it, add to it, and record it all in the records of his mind or his consciousness or whatever it was called.

Dave understood now; the reason the elephant was there was that everything was trying to see, perceive, or make sense of, things in the wrong direction. It didn't make sense unless you understood that the physical reality that we knew was being projected from within it, and part of something; something much larger, of which we are only seeing and understanding and perceiving the physical subset part of.

There was a flash of inspiration and the elephant had changed. It was now wearing a lab coat and a mad science professor wig. It started talking to him now in his head, indicating that his mind was getting more technical in explaining things to him.

It wasn't talking though, it was just knowledge loading itself into his head, sort of in parallel.

So if we only know what we know, i.e. what we understand and have experienced or seen throughout our lives, then you can only describe the concept of what this all is in relation to those things that you have knowledge of, even if this isn't like anything that you already know.

This was why there have been so many interpretations of it, in so many ways, throughout history. Mostly that is all we can cope with, understand, and it is for our own protection.

As we learn and understand more about everything so our collective perception changes, seeing it more in an unfiltered, unprotected, les naïve way.

We just have to get better at coming up with knowledge and understanding, use better descriptions, and see more of it, and the nature of how we exist.

The physical world we see and experience is just a tiny part of the information and energy available, yet that is the part with the driving capability for change; through random evolution, controls, laws, and energy.

In so doing it is building and growing minds within minds of evolving complexity within this encompassing evolving field structure, and it is all represented by the physical universal interpretation which is part of it, and which it has manifested into perception.

Dave shook his head, to try and clear his brain. It didn't work. His mind needed some props to help explain things.

On the far wall Dave noticed a curtain that he hadn't spotted before. He walked over to it, bent down on the floor and moved the curtain to one side with his beak. Behind the curtain he saw a little door made of wood, and the door had a little handle.

Luckily, as he was short of time, it didn't need a key, and he opened it and looked out into a field and landscape stretching off to the pink horizon.

The field was green, as you would expect, with all the blades of grass all the same length - almost plastic looking.

Little lollipop trees lined a perfect, white, picket fence; all unbelievably real, intense, and vibrant.

There was a stream with five hooded figures next to it, and a blue angel, and a sky full of stars, which was odd considering that it was daytime.

There was a sheep eating the plastic grass, and it stopped and looked up at Dave, "Alright Dave?" it said with a smile, in a rather elephant-like nasal tone. It grinned at him and nodded, which was somewhat disconcerting.

Dave slammed the door. *Ahhhh, Wrong sort of field* he thought.

You see... continued Dave's mind, *the fundamental problem is that it isn't something you can describe simply as a field, or as collective consciousness, or as a universal mind, a zeitgeist, a rhizome, a matrix, psyche bubbles within spheres, and so on.*

You can't currently show, or express, or demonstrate, or explain what it all is, by any means possible, from what we can currently see, hear, perceive, show, or visualise from the physical context.

Even if you use religious stories and New Age-like dreamscapes - you are still only trying to describe and define the major whole from within, and by, the language terminology and drawings of the physical minor part.

It is like trying to describe what gravity, and electromagnetic field, or say snow, actually is by just using what you can see, and to someone who has never felt it.

Dave could see why it had been easier in the ancient past to just give it an all-encompassing name, a non-defining generic term, and an all knowing, all seeing, universal name. It was easier.

Dave thought 'Mildred' would be a good choice instead.

...You can't say that it is 'like' anything that you can perceive. It isn't 'like' anything real or anything that you can imagine - what you see in the physical world is a reflection, a perception, the part that makes sense, that is necessary or useful to know.

It's like being in a universal computer program that has rules, and is a projected representation of information being processed - but there is a whole lot more to it than that - it is also alive, just as we are, but in a different way.

So there is no way of demonstrating or representing it with anything that you already know or understand, have heard, seen, or made sense of.

There are no mechanisms with which to define it. It's like trying to describe a film in a book of braille, which is a simple serial representation of a vast parallel context.

So that's the problem for penguins who have experienced it in any depth, who have tried to represent it, or spoken of what they have 'seen', or tried to work to understand. They have tried to express it in many terms and forms; stories, art, science, religions, films, books, biology, psychology, philosophy, music, quantum physics, and even with information technology.

It doesn't matter how hard you try with any of these areas, you will always end up with the elephant shortfall. You can still only base what you are experiencing on what you know and understand, hence all the historical interpretations and the creation of religions.

*Unless you have experienced it all for yourself, and on many levels over and over again, **and** you can apply knowledge and intelligence, you will never 'get it'; never put all the pieces together. You will always be trying to plug the gaps with ideas, thoughts, concepts, and suggestions from other people in the past.*

But then even 'getting it' doesn't seem to have any particular benefit attached to it anyway, aside from chaotic grief, the bruises and the sticky plasters.

So what we perceive as reality is in fact a projected subset of a much more detailed defining field or multi-levelled information structure that is representing it.

The physicality is a shadow of it, yet part of it, in effect a hologrammatical informational physical image of something much bigger, and on many more levels, and with vastly more information depth and complexity, most of which doesn't make any bloody sense to the physical part of 'us'.

But then that's what 'reality', or at least the physical reality that we have worked so hard to make sense of, is all about; bringing order and organisation and logic to the chaos, rational to the irrational, sense and order, perception of the truth through knowledge.

The only question, therefore, is **why?** *Aside from evolution and survival of course, what seems to be missing is any sort of direction, external drivers, something to evolve toward or compete against. Which also explains a lot of the mess in the physical world.*

Dave wanted to stop now. His brain was wandering off in the same direction as his stomach which hadn't had any food for several hours.

But his mind was still talking to him, busy working things out, and still repeating itself.

So… it went on, *in effect evolution is also happening within the field at the same time, and we are perceiving this evolution as a physical biological projection. Which is also manifesting change and recording the information within the 'field'. Which itself has rules constraints and laws in which to exist, and guide.*

This obviously all provides a mechanism for reverse engineering that quantum field as a bidirectional synchronised frequency resonance at many levels and in formed mental structures…

Dave's brain was nodding in agreement, but his mind had a slight concern that it may not be all going in, so it made a last ditch effort.

…Our physical interpretation therefore; what we see, hear, smell, touch, is simply an integrated aspect of part of the

information within the evolving organising consciousness field.

This gives structure and meaning and consequently probability to part of that field, the physical.

Which in turn evolves and allows the vast remainder to be programmed, even though it has no perceivable context, i.e. no space and time, that can be defined in physical or real terms and context.

That was enough.

This was really making Dave's brain hurt, and he was getting tired now as well as hungry.

So he decided it was time to go.

He lifted the needle off the record of his mind, and he turned to the elephant and thanked him politely, and started to climb back out of the hole which was now in a sort of spiral so it made it a bit easier, and thankfully, quicker.

A few hours later when he had got back home, he told everyone what had happened, and that they didn't have to worry as he had been to Haven and spoken with the elephant, and that he had managed to get safely out of his mind…

Which they were all surprisingly in agreement on, and nobody seemed to want to argue with him.

It took Dave several days for it all to sink in, to think, and work out what he had been shown.

Dave couldn't just ignore it all though, and he was determined that he was going to sort it all out, now. He had a plan.

He was going to go back and prod it with a sharp stick, a new sort of wake up 'symbol', and get it talking to more penguins, get it to do something, be more responsible, and then everyone would 'see' and be happier, hopefully.

He would also explain it all to everyone, and show how it 'talked' through synchronicity, and how it invoked global penguin organisational changes.

He would be able to explain how it all worked through quantum spin-structured brain programming, and how it mapped into biology and penguin brain structure, integrated with all the other mental and biological resonating structures.

That was all the first phase of 'The Plan'.

The next phase would be trying to do something about it all, moving it all forward in a coherent, shared benefit sort of way.

Plan B of course, was to put a lead bucket on his head, duct tape some protective crystals to his body (as more of a sort of statement really),

and then to run like hell…

7   DAVE'S CAT

Dave once had a pet cat.

He had bought it from a pet shop, much to the surprise of the owner, who, as his customers were all penguins, mostly sold just fish.

Dave had bought it to try out an experiment. He had got the idea for his experiment from a magazine article about a man called Schrödinger.

This guy had thought up an experiment with a cat in a box, where you didn't know if the cat was alive or dead or not, or something like that, and knowing the answer to the problem would mean answering the deepest mysteries of the universe.

It was a big problem in physics where particles didn't exist until you consciously perceived them, and it didn't make any sense to anyone. They had described it as the large awkward 'elephant in the room problem'. So Dave thought he could help.

So on the way to the pet shop, Dave had also picked up an unwanted cardboard box from the supermarket, one which was big enough for the cat to go in, and with no holes in it so that it couldn't cheat. He had asked at the supermarket for the other things needed in the experiment, a hammer, a bottle of poison, and some radioactive plutonium.

However, annoyingly, they were completely out of stock, which was probably due to them having a buy one get one free promotion the week before or something.

So he made do with a baited rat trap, and a lottery scratchcard glued to it to create the same sort of random effect.

He had popped them into his shopping trolley on his way round, which irritatingly seemed to veer off in different directions all the time, as if it had a mind of its own, which probably accounted for all the strange looks he was getting.

Perhaps they are just jealous he thought.

When he got back home, Dave had set it all up and had sat there quietly for an hour or two trying to work it all out; just staring at the box with the cat in it with the trap and the lottery card, or perhaps just at a box with no cat in it at all. In the time that he was thinking he also tried to think of a name for the cat, and as it was a male cat he decided to call it Dave.

Dave the Cat.

It was a really tough thing, trying to work out if the cat was dead, or not, or even if it was still in there. Eventually after two more hours he got fed up of waiting for the answer to arrive, and he quickly stuck his wing in under the lid, just to have a quick feel, to see if it was still in there and moving.

He had figured that without actually looking at it, without perceiving it, this would give him the information he needed without being conscious of it. He figured that if he did it fast enough, then the action wouldn't count as 'perceiving' it, and he would know the answer. He would sort of trick it, unsuspecting like, and get the information quickly and rapidly, without actually changing it, or disturbing it.

Sort of catch it unawares.

It had been a very long and embarrassing five hours in casualty, and Dave shuddered at the memory.

The worst of it had been explaining how it had happened to the doctor, along with the strange looks at him in the waiting room, with his best scarf wrapped around his wing. But mostly at the loud cardboard box next to him which growled warningly when even anyone came near it.

It was all fine until an old lady had come in with a little dog called Miffy. She had sat down and put Miffy on the seat next to Dave. Apparently Miffy had had become quite nervous and irritable after his operation two weeks before.

It had been a 'casteration', whatever that was, which was 'necessary' as he was becoming 'troublesome'. Miffy did look quite nervous and insecure.

The lady had asked Dave if he didn't mind if she opened the box, and say hello to his 'kitty'. Dave didn't mind, but unfortunately 'kitty' did, and Dave had to go back to the queue again while the doctors spent ten minutes detaching 'kitty' from her face.

Nature was a strange thing, and worked in very mysterious ways.

Miffy though looked quite pleased and excited at the incident for some reason. But then he looked sad again when the lady came back. Dave felt sorry for Miffy.

While she was away Miffy had told him conspiratorially, that the lady had given him the operation as part of the global demasculination control process that was going on, whatever that was, something to do with the competing female side of the collective mind.

Apparently she was very 'New Age', whatever than meant, and she was behaving this way in reaction to the male Jungian-style control psychology, which had in itself become a sort of religion, or collective control and belief structure.

This was also why apparently Jung was surrounded by powerful women who were trying to control him, and making sure he didn't do anything dangerous like breaking it, or stupid like seeing too much and really working it all out.

But Dave wasn't really into conspiracy theories, and he just smiled back politely.

Dave had read up quite a lot of psychology and philosophy stuff; Jung, Gebser, Deleuze, Sloterdijk, and even seen some very modern stuff on the Internet, and of course on 'Penguintube' where it was all made very obvious.

So he knew a lot about what was really going on, and what it all meant and how it all worked, and how easy it was to be drawn into assumptions about what it was all about.

You just had to see what had meaning, structure and logic, combined with scientific proof, and not get drawn along with too much of some of that psychobabble.

It wasn't all really his thing, he had just been driven by the need to find out what was going on and what it all meant, some understanding of what was happening to him and what was going on, without getting drawn into these new 'religions'.

Actually his 'religion' was more along the lines of fishing and sunbathing, and the structured management of doing what his wife asked him to do as quickly as possible so he could maximise time spent on the first two things.

They say that 'curiosity killed the cat', but Dave thought Miffy was hoping it would be the other way around.

Dave also thought it was strange how dogs had evolved; what had made them be what they were, what had made them change into what they had to be today.

Why did they behave so much like their owners, what did that say about them, and why had nobody thought about this?

To pass the time, Dave had started reading some of the magazines on the table in the waiting room. There was one which had an article on the new Mars Rover which was very interesting, Dave liked space things, and especially things on Mars.

This Rover was called *Curiosity*, which again was a strange coincidence.

There was another magazine which was called *Mindless Gossip* that the woman had been reading, and it seemed to be more of a comic with pictures of people. Dave couldn't help have a quick look through.

On the fifth page, along with lots of other adverts for things you may want but didn't need, like trousers, there was one for remote controlled collars, which were decorated with diamantes in a choice of colours from red to blue-white with LEDs, and there were even invisible ones.

Apparently the remote control was for training purposes, to give instructions and administer correction. The advert had a banner across it

Black Friday Special
Now with free bag of reward treats
for the little hero in your home.

Dave put the magazine down quickly, and was careful to avoid any eye contact.

The lady who 'owned' Miffy eventually came back. Luckily she didn't blame Dave and seemed to be quite polite about it all. She picked up a newspaper from the table and started to read it. Dave couldn't help looking over her shoulder.

The articles in the paper all seemed to be all about violence, politics, and worldwide chaos.

She eventually closed up the paper and started re-reading the front cover again; it was all about soap operas, explaining which TV, film, and sports stars were sleeping with who, what they were wearing, and who had operations to make them look strange.

"Isn't it terrible all this news?" said the woman putting the paper back down on the table and gesturing at it to Dave.

"Why is everything in such chaos, and why doesn't someone just do something about it all?"

She looked at Dave, Dave looked at Miffy, who gave him that 'See? I told you' and then that 'duhhh' exasperated look.

Any potential to cause change by this 'hero' had been effectively countered by a whole range of subtle and sophisticated control systems, from attitudes, chemicals, beliefs, and physical constraints.

It was hard to be a tall poppy when someone has cut your leaves off.

When it was eventually Dave's turn, the nurse was very kind and gentle bandaging his wing up, explaining that that sort of thing happened all the time and that this had been the third one that day. Which had made Dave feel a little better, she was very kind and Dave liked her a lot.

Dave looked down at the ground, sighed, and shuddered again in embarrassment.

Dave thought that the fundamental problem in general was perception; after all the cat knew it was in the box, it knew if it was alive or dead or not, and that knowledge was probably coming from the cat's mind. Probably the box knew too, and everything else around did as well.

It was just Dave that didn't, or perhaps he did, but he wasn't letting himself know, after all he didn't need to know everything.

So this view of reality that we had was somewhat fundamentally flawed. We were perhaps looking at everything in the wrong way, from the wrong direction, and only in part. He was trying to describe it all from one way, of what we knew, understood, and what we could perceive as physical reality.

Which obviously was a limited perception, a small piece of it all, from a narrow set of dimensional thinking. So with only one side of the story, you could only describe what the other side was like by what you knew, which was fine up to a point.

We were trying to organise it all, make sense of it from the wrong direction or context, when of course it didn't if you only had a limited scope.

There was perhaps a more complex reality of which we were only seeing part, a sort of reality within reality, of which we could only make part sense of and perceive, or only needed to, as the other larger part didn't or wasn't useful or have meaning, yet.

Perhaps it was all evolving together, one big system, one within another, all exchanging programming information, defining and influencing one other, and that it had all that had been going on for a long time.

Dave had also read another article in the magazine that said that everything was a hologram, and that everything could exist anywhere in the universe instantly, and that things only existed if you saw them with your mind, whatever that was, and wherever it lived.

It sounded like an odd way of looking at things, especially as they all obviously weren't everywhere.

If everything *was* a hologram or software or information, then we were only able to see things from that perspective, and in that context.

So when you went down to the basic binary code and pixels, there was nothing below that that made any sense.

Obviously that information was being created or projected from something else that did, something that was trying to make sense of itself, like iron filings in a field, that gave you the shape, direction and scope of a field as it changed and developed; but you couldn't actually see it, but it *was* there, and you were only seeing the shape of it.

But the field was not there to see - it was like gravity you couldn't see that – you could only perceive it by what it affected.

Dave liked gravity, he was very grateful for it, equally he liked the ground, they were both very much 'in the now' things, and you knew where you were with both of them.

It was probably where his mind was - in that field thing all around him like a bubble but with no time or space to it. It was translating part of itself into something he could see and feel, along with everything else. But not all at once. It probably knew the cat was in the box, as the cat was part of it, and the box too.

Perhaps it knew everything, or was just like some sort of mind operating framework, on which everything existed. If it knew about the cat he wished it had told him - told him if it was still there or not, and or, dead.

He rubbed his wing where it still ached from the memory; somehow it didn't feel like a hologram.

The next day he had taken the cat back to the pet shop and asked for a refund.

He explained that the problem was that the cat wasn't dead, it hadn't 'shuffled off its mortal coil', and worse than that, he could still see it, so it also hadn't 'ceased to be'. He had then waved his bandaged wing at the shopkeeper as evidence.

The shopkeeper was surprisingly friendly, and very quick to exchange the cat for some fish, he even helped Dave out of the door, and put some extra fish in his box free of charge.

The problem now was that Dave had to try and start thinking 'bigger'.

He had to put himself into something that had a bigger perspective, look at things from another direction, and think of things in a different way, outside physical reality, in a different way to that which he had evolved to do so in the past.

Which meant he was going to need a bigger box.

One that was big enough even for an elephant..

8 DAVE'S CHRISTMAS HAT

Dave didn't like Christmas. It wasn't that he had anything against it; it was just that he was expected to do so many things, and it was always a bit of a let-down, you know, always somewhat disappointing, overhyped, predictable?

He was supposed to get all excited for weeks beforehand; he was supposed to get presents and cards for people, relatives, even ones he didn't like. He was supposed to sing songs, eat too much, see the same old movies, and watch everyone else having a great time, just doing the same old thing year after year.

But not Dave. This year he just couldn't see the point.

Worst of all though, and this really was the most awful bit, he was supposed to wear his Christmas Hat; the red woollen itchy one, with the white pom-pom on the end of the pointless floppy cone. Every year it came out of the Christmas box.

Every year, he had to put it on, and every year he had to keep it on, for days.

Of course, it itched like mad, especially in the heat, and he looked really stupid in it.

He really hated that hat.

So Dave was not a happy bunny, and even though he didn't know what a bunny was, he was sure he wouldn't be a happy one. The only thing he knew about bunnies was that they lived down rabbit holes, and they lived in fear and ignorance, and were controlled by chemicals.

In any case he certainly wasn't one, and he certainly wasn't a happy penguin, that was for sure.

He could never understand what Christmas was all for, and why it was all during the hottest time of the year, when the sun never went down, so you couldn't sleep off the hangovers.

His wife seemed to love Christmas though; she would get all excited - looking forward to it all, wrapping presents, sending cards. Which to Dave was all a bit odd and pointless, as they saw all the same penguins every day anyway, so what was the bloody point.

She also spent a lot of time deciding what she was going to wear, and getting anxious if 'the big day' would all go 'OK', and everyone be 'merry'.

She always wanted everything to be 'just right', 'perfect', 'happy and jolly', spending almost all day putting up bits of coloured seaweed here and there, on bits of stupid driftwood. Which he had to help with, because it was 'traditional', oh and did he mention 'stupid'?

He had tried to work out why it had all started, and when it had all began, and what exactly was being celebrated. He asked his best mate –

"Well," said his mate "its traditional innit? You know one of them pagan festival fingies, wot sort of got taken over? All to mark the end of the year, and get rid of all the food, you know, and everyone hopes it will be a white Christmas?"

And he laughed.

Dave looked confused.

"Look, it's a laugh!!" His mate continued, "Something to get everyone together, have a bit of fun, a bit of a singsong, you know, tell a few stories, jokes, games, dancing that sort of fing - catch up on some gossip. Nuffin' wrong with that is there?"

And he looked at Dave questioningly.

Dave wasn't so sure though, and after several hours of asking around, nobody could really give him a proper answer. It seemed that nobody knew why they were doing it, or what it was really for.

But of course, in doing so he had also made everyone else think about it, and he had started to make people worry, and now he was also worried; worried that he may be turning into a bit of a grouch.

So he just got on with it, and went with it for the next few days.

So the night finally came - well it wasn't really a night more of a slightly less intense bright glare - everyone was ready, and all the little penguins and chicks were busy trying to pretend to be asleep.

It was at that point, when it was all quiet, that Dave decided to wander off to get some peace. To try and think things through a bit, on his own.

He walked away from the colony, and up one of the small hills at the base of the mountain that overlooked the valley of the penguins.

He wanted to be away from everyone, to have a bit of space, to rest, and not be in danger of waking up with a red nose wedged on the end of his beak, and being surrounded by sniggering, pesky chicks.

He made a last check around, leaned with his back

against the rocks, looked over the whole valley for a moment, gave a sigh, and then closed his eyes.

Then, no more than a few moments later there was an awkward cough next to him. Dave didn't open his eyes, he was too scared, nobody ever came up here but him.

"Blimey, it's cold out here" said the voice.

Then there was another voice that came from to Dave's other right, "You're telling me" said the other voice. Dave opened his left eye and caught sight of a ghostly penguin figure next to him.

The ghost penguin was all in white, with a white light around his head. Dave wasn't frightened at all, even though this was the first ghost he had ever seen. The ghost penguin looked at him and nodded and continued to blow virtual hot breath in-between his transparent flippers as he rubbed them together.

"Who are you?" asked Dave.

The ghost puffed himself up and waved his flippers around expansively, and spoke in a deep, echoing voice. "I am the penguin Ghost of Christmas Past, and I am here to show you your life and what you have done wrong until now, and why you are so bad, bitter and cold-hearted, even though so many people have helped you."

Dave looked worried. "What should I call you?" asked Dave tentatively. "You can call me 'IT' if you like - everyone else does."

"Here we go!" said the ghost and there was a *whoosh* in the air, and then – nothing. "There you go, that didn't take long did it?" asked the ghost.

Dave looked very confused.

"Now I will pass you on to my colleague on your right, the penguin Ghost of Christmas Present." Dave looked to his right, and there was another ghost standing there; but this one was much larger, rounder, jollier, and more colourful, and was busily tucking into a tray of sushi.

"Hang on…" said the Ghost of Christmas Present, his mouth full of fish and rice, "Be with you in a minute. That went a bit quick sorry, wasn't expecting you back so soon"

Then, before anyone could say anything the wind changed and became quite chilly – which was going some. The air took on a feel of darkness and oppressiveness, the same as Dave had once felt when he was a small boy waiting outside the Headmaster's office.

Then another ghost appeared in front of him, but old, withered, and fearful. Dave looked sideways to the first ghost but he had vanished, and so had the second one, along with the sushi.

"Dave," came the voice from the last ghost "I am the penguin ghost of Christmas Future. I am here to show you what will happen to you if you do not change, if you do not become a better penguin and mend your ways. You have been shown what you have done wrong, and why that is bad, and you have been shown what that has led to today and what people think of you. Now I will show you what will become of you if you stay on that path."

Dave raised his wing, and gestured with it to ask the obvious question, but the figure just ignored him and carried on with his script.

"If you carry on the way you are, in the future, you will be alone, cold, on your own on a beach, just you, with nothing to do, with nobody wanting to talk to you, is that what you want…… is that what you really, truly want….?"

Dave didn`t know what he wanted, of course he didn't want to be alone but he did like peace and quiet.

"Ummm…" said Dave "Well actually…" but the ghost interrupted him again.

"You must change Dave, you must become a better penguin, not be such a grouch, go forth and help others, work hard, share and give all your fish away. You must become a better penguin, and then you will find happiness."

Dave still looked very confused - it didn't make a lot of sense. Then a cloud appeared, transparent and misty, which lifted them both up into the air and carried them to the penguin graveyard at the bottom of the mountain.

The ghost then gestured towards a small pile of loose rocks. "This ….. Dave, is what you will become if you do not change, just a forgotten pile of rocks that nobody cares for."

It made Dave feel very sad, very lost and alone. He wanted to change, be more, be a better, harder working, caring penguin, it made him very sad indeed, and guilty.

It was then that he looked sideways to a large marble obelisk just to the left of the rocks.

Dave the Saviour Penguin was written on it in big carved letters, and there were many brightly coloured stones at its base, and bits of fine seaweed laid carefully in front of it.

The ghost looked at Dave. "Ignore that - it belongs to another Dave, not you."

Dave looked a bit further up the obelisk and there was a big picture of Dave in a frame higher up on one side; he was wearing a medal and holding a Nobel Prize, and there were lots of girls names scrawled in lipstick next to the picture.

Standing on the top was a large statue of Dave, it was unmistakably him, but they clearly hadn't quite got his side profile quite right - some of the features were clearly a little 'overdone', and clearly 'six-packs' were very tricky to do in marble.

"So now you have seen, now you understand" said the ghost gesturing towards the pile of rocks. Then he began ushering the confused Dave back onto the cloud before he could say anything.

He was clearly pleased that the point had been made. The cloud lifted up and they returned to the rocky hillside, and back to the present day.

"So you see" said the ghost, "Unless you change your ways you will become nothing more than a lonely pile of rocks that nobody remembers, and nobody visits or cares about. You will be forgotten. You must change, feel guilty and do something."

Why was everything always trying to get me to change, thought Dave, *do things, be something else?*

There was a great expansive *whooshing* noise, and the ghost vanished, but just before he did, there was an expression on his face that indicated that there may have been the slightest of chances that he may have received the wrong memo, or picked up the wrong file on the way out of the office, and delivered the wrong speech to the wrong penguin ?

Which of course never happens.

Dave felt worse after the visit from the three ghosts; he hadn't done anything wrong, he didn't want to change, and as far as he could see it was everyone else that was the problem.

He walked back to the colony and was greeted by all his friends, and then his wife, who seemed very excited.

"I have a surprise for you" she said. She took out a piece of mistletoe from behind her back. "I found it washed up on the beach a few days ago."

She raised it up and kissed him – he was very surprised, and he smiled. The mistletoe must have been carried a long way by the sea, and from a land very far off, it was a miracle how it had arrived here.

Then he understood what it was all about, he understood the message that had been carried a long way from distant shores. Or at least how it was interpreted and transferred.

The love - that was what it was all about - that was what was important. Just penguins coming together to remember to love each other, that was what mattered nothing else really.

Despite everything, it was love that mattered, and what could be more important than that?

Except that obviously Dave drew the line at his mother-in law, after all there had to be rules and limits...

...even at Christmas..

9 THE SAVIOUR PENGUIN

It was a complicated system, this evolutionary business, on many levels - and not just the physical world but also within the spiritual quantum consciousness field thingy – or wherever it was that all the penguin programming information came from.

'The Messiah Penguin'... thought Dave *...there was always a clue in the job title, in this case the first bit. Sort of like 'crash test dummy', as with most of these sort of jobs you don't just have to read the small print, to get a clue of what was involved.*

The problem was that he wasn't really the Messiah 'saviour' Penguin, as in the *Life of Brian* film he was 'just a naughty little penguin', just as his mother had always told him he was.

It was merely a case of mistaken identity, and the collective penguin consciousness had obviously got it wrong.

More likely it had come up with the idea of what he should be subconsciously from all those films, books, and needy thoughts and wishes everyone had.

It was just waiting for some fool to come along and sign up to the 'Saviour' Job Description; some idiot, some gullible muggins to fall into the usual 'Saving the Penguin World' hero trap.

Besides the role sort of required a selfless nature, putting yourself last, losing your ego, and sacrificing everything for 'the cause'. Which Dave wasn't very good at.

For starters he was rather attached to his 'self', and if he had an ego somewhere, then he was sure it would be a large one and subsequently, one worth keeping.

It was all very well experiencing all of those synchronistic events, having knowledge, events pointing to him, all those people writing about him and prophesising about him, but it was more likely that it was all part of trying to convince him to take the bait, trying to make him think he was 'the one', getting him to somehow believe he was 'the chosen 'Saviour' penguin'.

Which of course he wasn't.

He wasn't falling for that one, not even if the bait was a large barrel of fish. He wasn't signing on the dotted line of any virtual contract, and then just end up becoming another religious cliché.

Oh no, not him, not *ever*.

No, it was just a whole range of ideas and thoughts that other people had had over history that it was trying to manifest into form, trying to make happen, trying to get someone to live the dream, be the hero.

If he was the 'Messiah' penguin he would have been told, shown what to do, or, at the very least asked, but he hadn't, so he wasn't, and that was that.

The trouble was though that he knew everything; he knew what had to be done, he could see things that others couldn't, he saw everyone in a different way, and it all made him feel responsible, awake to the problems and what was going on.

This was a problem, or a kind of dilemma, but only if he knew what that actually meant.

But from Dave's point of view, he was just a penguin, what difference could he make? He wasn't going to stand up on some hill or rock, and tell everyone what to do, with a glowing aura about his head.

With everyone expecting him to be saying all the right things, flashing his white teeth, his electrifying charisma and personality, inspiring everyone, and somehow making everything OK.

It just wasn't going to happen, his mind couldn't be everywhere at once, and the collective penguin mind had to come to terms with that. Just to make it clear, he folded his wings in front of him and shook his head.

The trouble with that again though, was that being a Messiah Penguin or Prophet Penguin, a 'Saviour for a time', or whatever he was supposed to have been was a bit of a dying breed and concept really.

It was now all about thinking, influencing the collective mind, doing all the work, getting all that knowledge, coming up with new stuff, and getting everyone to do things.

Which made it was more than a bit tough going these days, intense, and somewhat life threatening.

Also it sort of made you, well, a bit boring frankly, and poor, and not very exciting, not to mention difficult to understand.

Also if you were to say or do the wrong thing at the wrong time, everyone would just have a go at you, even though you knew you were right, after all, you could only do so much. The whole thing was a bit like a penguin trying to tow the *Titanic*.

So naturally, girls too thought you were a bit weird, boring, and not very exciting, which of course made having more messiahs and prophets tricky. In fact it made the whole process kind of difficult to reproduce – as it were - a sort of reverse feedback problem, brought on by lack of external planetary evolutionary pressure or guidance.

You were much more likely to get more penguins that were the opposite, you know - exciting, flamboyant, charismatic, rich, entertaining, but all in a useless sort of way, but still popular with the penguin girls. The girls, after all were the ones that held the evolutionary ropes, and knew what they wanted, or at least thought they did. So not surprisingly everything was given somewhat of a bias towards the 'what was wanted', rather than 'what was needed', which in both cases lacked any form of overall strategy or plan.

As a result getting the collective penguin mind to change, evolve, be something more, was kind of tricky, especially when it didn't want to, and made it hard for you to even try; reacting against you with its own perspective and subconscious objectives, when it didn't even know what it was itself.

It was like trying to get some giant mindless bureaucratic organisation to change, which would make life very difficult for you and react against you, attacking you, unconsciously like a machine. So any time you tried to get it to do something it didn't like, even it was wrong in itself, and in trouble, it would resist you.

It would avoid doing anything, go round in circles, anything rather than what it was supposed to do and becoming very devious and clever at doing it. But of course individual penguins never behaved like that.

So the possibility of there being other penguins being able to do what he did, and see what he saw and did, was less and less likely, and the circumstances for them to be able to do what he did, and to have someone like his wife with him, helping him and taking care of him along with others, well that was almost impossible.

Almost, but not quite – especially if there was a big fundamental problem, and Dave thought about the *Titanic* again in the film of it he had seen.

But Dave wasn't a Messiah Penguin or a Prophet Penguin, or the Saviour. He didn't glow in the dark or hear voices from a penguin god in his head, he was just an ordinary penguin who had accidentally seen too much, and worked too much out.

It was unfortunate, but that's the way it was.

In fact the whole thing and experiences had more than ruffled a few of his feathers, which took quite a lot these days, for a 'rufty tufty' bloke penguin, that he knew he was.

If anything, he saw himself as a sort of manager or director penguin, yes 'manager', that was a good definition as it didn't mean that he had a label that someone else had created. It didn't have great expectations attached to it, but it also meant it sounded as though he was qualified (which of course he wasn't).

The trouble with the Messiah or Saviour role was that it didn't really have a Job Description; everyone wanted there to be one, but nobody could define what they would have to do, how or what it was that was meant to be done, or by when. Let alone what they should look like - all the skills, the capabilities, and charisma.

The role and objectives for the task weren't that very well defined either, i.e. 'Save Everyone' - from what exactly? 'Describe how everything was all a mess and what it needed to be instead', 'What was causing all the problems?' - Those sort of clear and well defined objectives. Or was there some sort of plan that had to be followed or delivered? Or were you supposed to come up with your own plans?

It just wasn't clear at all.

Having a 'glow in the dark' head, being popular, and able to do miracles wasn't really a very good CV requirement, and could be fulfilled by most glow-worms. But the 'manager' title sounded much better.

It did though make him sound a bit boring, so other penguins would be more likely to leave him alone, and he could get on with his job, rather than being strung up or stoned.

He could also use one of those black folders and go to meetings, whatever they were. He would also have a *Plan*, and he would just have to think of things, get ideas, put them into the Plan and they would miraculously get done, somehow, as they always did.

Problems would just arrive, he would 'see' what needed to be done, make decisions, and then it would al happen, somehow, probably.

Dave was also different. Dave was smart, and he knew that if he was going to change things, which of course he wasn't, he would have to be both a manager and a good bloke penguin.

This, in his mind, was lucky, as coincidentally he was both, and he was good at those things too.

Balance both sides, manage himself, look after himself, do a good job in a balanced, shared benefit way, for both sides. No problem, except that *he wasn't doing it*, and he had to remind himself of that fact again.

His head started to ache, and something was also playing with his mind. It started hurting on the top of his skull again, so he tried to think about something else.

It seemed that penguins had evolved gradually away from needing to influence the collective penguin mind, even though they had clearly seen it and were heavily influenced by it.

Which probably meant that it had the upper hand, like an ant colony that didn't need to change, because it had everything provided for it, and existed in its own evolutionary bubble. Penguins didn't really care, as long as there were fish, and it wasn't too cold, too crowded, and they had mates, of both sexes, they were fine, everything was OK.

Of course there were no radio signals here, no electrical interference, no chemicals, only fresh pure ice water and fish. It was easy enough to perceive the collective penguin mind here, see what was going on, here in the remote part of the Antarctic. They even had fibre optic cables for the low emission TV sets, and there was no need for mobile phones, as everyone was within waddling distance - well eventually.

So when everything was fine here, nothing needed

to change. If nothing was wrong you didn't need to fight, if everything was organised, straightforward and working, you didn't need to adapt.

You would only need to do something like that if all the fish disappeared, or all the ice melted, or the air became poisoned.

Which of course would never happen, as they would never do anything to affect that.

No of course not, they weren't that stupid.

So why did he feel so strongly that he needed to do something? Why was he bothering?

He clearly didn't need to do anything, and he was more likely to just upset the other penguins. He couldn't get them to understand anyway, respond, or see things that he could see.

It was almost as if they were being deliberately prevented from seeing him, or from hearing what he was saying, or understanding his perspective, like they were in little controlled programmed bubbles of belief that they didn't need to come out of unless they were made to.

They didn't want to change unless something pushed them out of their protective comfort zones. There was some sort of beguiling force at work, keeping them blind inside their bubbles, hypnotised, and it kept them oblivious and protected in their day-to-day habits and routines, which generally was ok.

Frankly if they couldn't see what he knew, and if the collective penguin mind was the same, and was only interested in its short term perspective, what chance did he have in doing anything about it all?

Just because he had somehow managed to work

out a way to communicate with it through meaningful synchronic events, and to partly influence it in times of stress with collective actions, that wasn't going to get around the fundamental problems.

So somehow he had to get to the root of the problem, start putting more of the pieces together, make more sense, and get everyone to be more conscious of it, and do something inspirational.

He stopped and thought for a moment about the word he had just used, words always had deeper meanings to them, and operated much in the same way as computer languages did.

So he had to be motivated, and very clever, and try a few things that no other penguin had ever tried before

He narrowed his eyes and put his determined face on.

He was going to need another very large sharp stick, and he boldly set off towards the beach where no penguin had gone before.

To see if he could find one.

10 THE PENGUIN CINEMA

The local penguin cinema had come on a long way since Dave was young.

Originally, a very long time ago, it had started off being in a cave somewhere with just drawings and torches, but that had got a bit limited and cramped.

So everyone had moved outside to an open area marked around with stones, in which they had various talks and shows.

Then due to the weather, someone came up with the bright idea of having it all enclosed again but this time in a building with solid walls, where everyone just got together to talk and listen about stuff.

The room would probably be a bit dark, but at least it would be large enough so that everyone could sit down facing forward listening to whoever was standing up at the front, or have a singsong without shivering, and enjoy a bit of food.

Then after many years, someone had the bright idea of putting a screen up on the table at the front, onto which you could project images of things they liked to see. You could understand things more easily, talk about them, and agree ideas.

Then when Dave was a juvenile penguin things really got going when his uncle had got out his projector, and came up with the idea of having regular slide shows, which were mostly black and white images from his past. But it was entertaining, and something to focus the mind on.

Then the projector evolved, and movies came. They were a bit limited at first, but then came sound, and then colour. Then 3D arrived, which meant they all had to sit there with funny little glasses on.

It was all still a bit restricted though; you only really got a small perspective view of what was actually going on.

True reality, even with surround sound, or with water sprayed at you, or smells, and having the floor move, was still only about 1% of the information of reality that you could get over to everyone, even with the technology and bandwidth that had evolved so far.

But he supposed there were limits to what was able to be translated into something that rationally and logically made sense, from everything that was. A sort of bandwidth and organising problem.

Mind you, the rate of change of the technology was increasing very quickly now, almost every week there was something new. Not just new films with novel ideas, but newer and better ways of seeing them - getting more and more of the whole experience.

This then allowed you to see things in different ways. It obviously helped of course knowing what you were supposed to be looking at, and what it meant. Otherwise it was kind of pointless, or meaningless, like a goldfish watching the television.

The thing Dave really didn't like though was that it wasn't just the cinema that was changing technically, but also the films. They were getting much too extreme, sort of 'in-your-face'.

He liked the old films, the emotional black and white ones - the ones with feeling and good story lines. They seemed somehow more real, and with actors and actresses that could genuinely act, with charisma, and true emotion.

With the old films, as with reading books, you used your mind to enter into it, used your imagination.

Not these days. All the gaps were filled for you, and you didn't have to think or use your mind at all.

So these days it was all about the ride; the sensual rollercoaster, the violence and horror, the swearing, and needless rudeness. You sort of became desensitised to the emotions.

The films weren't clever any more, totally losing the connection with real penguins, the community feel; it just wasn't all there anymore.

Music was going the same way too, less emotional, less real somehow. Less fidelity, all noise and millions of small MP3's, rather than high quality live analogue full range quadraphonic that Dave's old stereo had. That's why Dave had hung on to his old record player too, and vinyl LP's; it wasn't just an emotional attachment, he also liked to remember how things sounded.

Yet the sound in the cinema seemed to be very good, though different from the music on MP3 players, which seemed to be getting less real, less true, which was odd.

The cinema that Dave found himself in today had evolved again. It boasted the new total immersion skin suits, and surround bubbles.

You were immersed into the 'experience', such that all your body senses were fed information at the same time and you were completely shut off from reality.

You had to wear a touch sensory skin suit inside the bubble or sphere, with a transparent, virtual reality headset, and surround sound headphones. So, inside your own bubble you had images projected onto it from inside it by the headset.

The whole thing then rolled around inside a large bubble-like round room with all the other penguin-bubbles interacting like some giant *Star Trek* 'holodeck' thing, that had been filled full of zorb balls all wirelessly networked together.

The images from flash memory that everyone were seeing, were all then produced and coordinated and projected onto the inside surface of each bubble, and into the room and walls.

The bubbles also had the ability to move around on the floor and bump into each other, and interact. There was also the ability to connect them together wirelessly if you wanted to, or hard wire a direct linkage if you really felt like it.

So the penguins were getting information from everywhere, which was limited only by what the system could cope with, and what the penguins could take in; sort of immunised to some extent from seeing everything in the cinema itself.

All the flashing lights and confusing mass of information was filtered into something that made conscious sense to everyone. It was all a pixelated, digital representation, or quantised view, of reality - both reading and writing data to and from everything.

It was all written in one go as a structure, to experience as a story, which was refined by what people thought of it. Sort of the other way around to how things really were, an objective view of how we were seeing, or perceiving things, and information with our minds and bodies.

Crazy stuff really.

After all, if you were trying to simulate the real world, you know actual reality, there would be no point in trying to produce it in any other way. You had to, in effect, create a physical framework environment to translate and generate one.

It was a massively complex virtual data system, an interpretation of information, projecting it, or parts of it in the best way you could, in a way that made sense. The only way of doing that was to create a software and hardware viewing sensory system that was in effect integrated with itself.

When penguins first arrived at the cinema they had to line up, and were then given a skin suit, which was fitted to them and connected up to their bubble at various points. Your bubble was then inflated, and then you were sort of shoved into the main giant cinema room, all ready to go.

You then had to pick the film up, or whatever was playing, as you went along, and try and make sense of it somehow, and join in and add to the experience.

It was a bit mad really, and the technology was clearly having trouble coping with the amount of data now flowing around.

The pictures would quite often stop, get pixelated or get out of step. But hey that was penguin technology for you, and if it didn't do that occasionally you might actually forget it was a hologram.

It was fun though, and you got a regular break when everything went dark, so you could rest, while the system updated itself.

It was interesting to see how technology changed, and what was popular, and what wasn't.

Dave remembered, with a slight grimace, his Betamax video player – unwrapped in its original packaging- up in his attic, along with several of these large LP-sized laser disks; "You never know - they may be valuable one day…" his wife had told him with a smile.

He remembered that he had read about it all in a gadget magazine in a barber shop.

They were the 'latest thing' at the time, except that he hadn't noticed that the magazine was 5 years out of date.

He wondered why it had all been so cheap when he placed his order on the phone, and why they were so keen to sell them to him, even giving him a free *Evangelists Today* magazine subscription for a year, which sadly was also backdated - so it didn't seem much of a consolation.

Dave looked around in the room, and he noticed that some of the suit bubbles were distinctly clouded over, *they're in their own little worlds* he thought.

Dave wasn't sure what they were seeing inside, or if they could pick up anything on the main screen at all, but hopefully they were having a nice time too.

The idea with all of it was that the films were now interactive, and you could consciously change the story or the characters by thinking through, and into the system, through the cables.

Sort of thinking outside of the bubble, and affecting what happened to you in the story and to others.

You could even physically move the pixels around to change what was displayed and how, but that took quite a bit of energy; most people were happy just to watch and be involved.

All of the penguins were all plugged into one system in the room that was all interconnected – well that was the idea anyway. There were always a few that just didn't get the idea or didn't want to join in the game, and just stayed on the side-lines watching whatever they were seeing in their own spheres, which was fine.

The whole cinema room, holodeck, hologram projector thing was limited by rules, laws, limits and constraints. This was obvious really, and for everyone's safety, and also so that it made sense.

You couldn't just do anything - you were physically limited by a number of things, which was sensible otherwise it wouldn't be any fun or point.

Today they were all watching *Happy Feet*, again, while everyone waited for the next David Attenborough natural history documentary to be released.

Dave did his best to join in, even though he had seen it dozens of times. Half way through the film it occurred to Dave that whoever was running the cinema, or selected the films and the environment, had quite a lot of control over what penguins saw, felt, and thought.

Mostly this was obviously decided by the penguins

themselves, the old 'bums on seats' principal, and all that. The same laws seemed to apply to what was available to buy and eat in the foyer.

But there was a certain direction or strategy at work, over and above all that. It was curious, and he wondered why nobody had questioned it all, or wondered why, and more importantly how it had turned out this way. Just in the same way as the Eloi people behaved in The Time Machine.

In the middle of one of the dance routines that everyone was joining in on, Dave realised that his bubble had a small leak somewhere, and that it was getting a bit sort of saggy.

He had a feeling that they had given him the wrong size body suit, it was labelled as **Large,** but it was clearly not the case, as it was far too tight in certain places.

The straps that connected his body suit to the bubble were complaining a bit too, and the one at the top started to make a rip in the bubble itself above his head.

There was a fault; suddenly the entire movie flashed in front of his eyes in just a few seconds. The screen on the inside of the bubble around him flickered for a moment, then it went blue….

Ahhh… thought Dave, just the same as on his laptop, it was the 'screen of death'.

Then a message appeared in front of him ….

Connection lost - synchronicity failure - dumping core to host cloud – report logged with operating system – Have a nice day - sorry.

There was a load ripping noise, and Dave had burst his bubble. "Uh oh…" he said quietly to himself, "I'm in trouble…", and he slumped onto the dark floor.

Feeling quite odd now, he took his interactive virtual reality helmet off, and climbed out of his skin suit, which was shaped to fit his six-pack. He unzipped the top of his now very floppy bubble, and climbed out onto the black electro-responsive floor.

It was a very odd feeling this 'out of bubble' experience, and it felt strange looking down on the suit and bubble he had been in, now just lying on the floor below him.

He looked around and saw all the other penguins in their bubbles bouncing around, enjoying themselves, all with their own personal spaces; All seeing the film playing, reacting to certain events and images, all at the same time, well mostly.

The bubbles would bounce around at points when things got quite exciting, although clearly some of the penguins were seeing some things slightly differently, or had different takes on what was being shown. However he wasn't part of it now, and neither was his bubble suit.

It felt as if he had come out of something, just like the 'better than life" game he had seen his favourite sci-fi series Red Dwarf, in which the players didn't know they were inside a virtual reality game.

That is until they worked it out, and sort of woke up into reality and removed their interactive headsets.

Dave was often worried that his whole life might be like that, some sort of virtual role playing game, and that he hadn't done very well in it. Missed something in the game that he should have done, or something obvious that he should have worked out. Like say how to defeat polar bears, or found the right magical symbols.

He always had that feeling he had missed out on something, not visited the right places, missed some clue, not read the right books, or was it because he lied when he was 17.

But of course he wasn't, and he hadn't, he had worked out everything, and had done everything right. It was just that the game was badly written, and being run on dodgy hardware.

He was also worried that all the girls in the game already knew all the rules, the gameplay, the cheat cards, and they were there just to wait for the male players to get it all too, watching them, steering them, and making sure they didn't do anything dangerous or stupid, that might break the system.

They certainly seemed to know a lot more than he did about what was going on.

But he was wrong there too.

Dave was also seeing things differently out of his bubble; and he now had a very odd perspective, seeing reality like this. It was also very tempting to just climb back into his bubble, and hide, or sleep.

He looked at his suit and bubble for a moment - he was a bit worried about just wandering off and leaving it for someone else to just walk into and use and then he remembered the tuna curry he had had the night before, and he suspected it would be a while before anyone would venture in past the firewall he had created.

He decided to go for a walk and explore this new environment - he had never seen all of this before - but instead of going back to the foyer he went through the **NO ENTRY** door to the side, and straight into the side street, from which there was light shining in from the cold blackness.

It was dark and raining. All along the main street, which was miles long, there were other cinemas everywhere.

Opposite him was an old Victorian cinema that looked to be falling apart, on the doorway it had the word **Condemned** written on it.

There was a short queue of very pale strange looking birds standing outside and they didn't have any umbrellas.

Dave looked up and the sign above the entrance had the words

'Now sh wing - *It's A W nderful L fe'*,

and above that, in large letters that were built into the building, were the words

DODO CINEMA

That was Dave's favourite film, he had it in his own DVD collection, it was a shame the cinema was closed now though.

Dave wondered why that had happened, and why there was still a queue. His video and DVD collection was not what you might call extensive, he only tended to buy DVDs if they really meant something to him, or if he wanted to watch something over and over again.

Someone once said that his mind was like a book, and you could read it like a book, but Dave thought it was more like a video library, a set of dreams or experiences that were recorded films.

Dave had a very simple video library, and very nice happy films, mostly from the '70's and early '80's. There was nothing in there that was inappropriate, which was probably more to do with the fact that he couldn't reach the top shelves in the video store.

He didn't have any horror ones, violent ones, rude ones, or angry ones, or any with bad language in. Mind you he did keep a secret stash of *Pingu* DVD's that his wife didn't know about - he had at least a small amount of rebel left in him.

In Dave's mind everything had started to go wrong sometime in the 1980's, almost gone backwards to an older form of world consciousness; flatter, less real, less depth and structure to it. Somehow nothing was real these days; it was all artificial, lacking reality, depth, meaning and feeling.

It was all too controlled, limiting, confining and compressed. It was the same for so many things - films, songs, books, Internet, people, even art. Even though the technology had developed in leaps and bounds.

What was being shown, and the imagination required to see it, were now both sadly limited. Where had it all gone? Where was the bright future, and why had it changed?

Or perhaps it was just him. Whatever it was - he missed it.

He shuddered in the dark rain and then looked left down the street. There were a lot of older cinemas down there, many of which still seemed to be busy, all showing the same old films. Apart from one which was showing *Jurassic Park* - that particular cinema had been closed down due to something large falling onto its roof, and it partly catching fire.

Dave wasn't that interested though - he didn't like horror films, they were a bit childish and gave him nightmares.

This street must sure have some memories, he thought to himself.

To the right, and way up the street, there were a lot of much bigger, newer cinemas; one was a giant multiplex complex on many storeys with dozens of screens in it, showing lots of films all at the same time. It was all brightly lit up.

Dave started walking that way up along the pavement, taking care not to get trodden on underfoot.

Now that he was closer, Dave could see that the main multiplex seemed to be showing all the same film story, just in lots of different ways, for different languages, cultures, and genres. It was a very busy and popular cinema with a lot of very tall penguins, or so it seemed from here, going in and out all the time.

As he got closer he recognised them as human beings, and this was their cinema complex. He walked up to the entrance, above which in the air were some very big cables coming in and out.

The foyer was very busy; crowds everywhere, full of people, but all very pale and ghostlike. It looked quite out of place though against the natural nostalgic feel of the rest of the street, and the people coming out looked a lot less happy than the ones going in, which was not a good sign.

Dave looked up into the air and the lights flashing from the street were reflected into the sky, which itself now looked like one giant bubble. However you could still see the stars in the night above shining through, which was quite reassuring somehow.

You could almost make out the shape of the all-powerful great Giant Purple Squirrel, which as everyone knew, we were all a part of and elements of its collective oneness.

It was so obvious; he couldn't understand why everyone couldn't see it. But you couldn't just tell everyone, some people probably thought it was still green, and you didn't want to offend them - and everyone else, well they may all say it was indigo, and that he was wrong or didn't have the complete picture, or it was only part of a much larger squirrel somewhere bigger and further out, and more complicated.

He looked at it again, it was almost hypnotic, it made so much sense though, and it was so logically flawless here, in this out-of-bubble world.

He then unprofessionally looked sideways, straight into our camera lens, raised his eyebrows and grinned, as if sharing some private joke or understanding with us, as the audience or viewers. Which kind of fell a bit flat, and made him look a bit of an idiot, which wasn't difficult.

He shook his head resumed his role, and then stepped into the foyer casually, and 'mingled', trying to look like he was meant to be there. Which of course, he was.

There were thousands of people wandering around inside, but they didn't notice him. It may have been his height, or maybe the fact that he was so odd that they couldn't see something that was so out of place.

However it was more likely they were more interested in seeing what was being streamed, and getting into queues.

Dave stared around in amazement at all the bright colours, flashing lights, noise and smells. There were just so many bright neon lights, and LEDs everywhere.

Dave had no idea why they needed so much intense lighting, with so many high energy photons being generated, maybe they wanted to be kept awake all night, and eventually becoming blind with irradiated retinas ?

There was a large counter there which seemed to be supplying food, all different colours and shapes and chemical odours, most of which was blue or like salty polystyrene. It was just like the stuff that got washed up on the beach, but people seemed to be eating it.

Dave screwed his face up, it was very unnerving.

The drinks seemed to be all different colours too, *they must have run out of water or something*, he thought. *You wouldn't get penguins eating and drinking that rubbish - not if they were in their right minds anyway.*

At the back there were escalators going up and down in all directions which led to a multitude of cinema rooms. At the ticket office there was a very long queue of human beings lining up to get their skin suits and bubbles.

Dave wasn't interested in seeing whatever films that had to show here - it all looked very mad and illogical - not to mention violent.

He did though decide to have a quick look in one of the cinema rooms; he walked over to the double doors and took a peek inside.

It was too dark for him to see anything clearly, but it was vast inside with bubbles grouped together inside bigger bubbles all floating around the bubble-shaped room, very similar to the penguins one but vastly more sophisticated and technical.

There must be dozens like this in this cinema Dave thought. The voice coming from inside the room sounded very nice though, sort of smooth and comforting, talking about things for their benefit, joy, comfort and pleasure, while soft gentle music played.

"I say, I say…" came a posh woman's voice from behind him. Dave jumped. "I say - actually, I think you'll find there is a queue, you know?" Dave turned round in surprise to find that there was a large, middle-aged woman walking straight towards him, with her hand raised looking at Dave, trying to get his attention.

Dave froze. He wasn't expecting that.

"I say, I think you will find there is a *queue*" she said more assertively this time as she approached him, putting more emphasis on the word 'queue', and pointing back to where she had come from. Dave leaned sideways, and looked past her to where the queue was now shuffling forward, filling the gap she had just made, oddly just in the same way that penguins did.

She then looked down at him "But you're a pen…" she said squinting at him in a confused manner. *Obviously short-sighted* he thought.

Then she turned around to look in the direction that Dave was looking, and at her now non-existent position in the queue. The look of horror came to her face, and she turned and dashed back waving her arms, and shouting forlornly trying to get back her place, gesturing to the totally non-interested queue.

Nature is a funny thing, thought Dave. Evolution and nature was at work everywhere.

The queue was very long indeed, which was strange as there were several open ticket desks. To Dave it just seemed to be mindlessly bureaucratic and illogical, with everyone needlessly queueing in the one line. It was something he couldn't stand, the mentality, the system of control at work, with the 'this is how it is' and 'red tape' mind.

There were several other people behind the counters, why weren't they selling tickets ?

Not their job, he thought, they were the "information", the "VIP reception" the "complaints" the "moving bits of paper around" people. He had seen this before in many unaccountable 'state' run organisations, 'just doing their job'. All looking busy, but in realty just waiting to politely turn back and belittle anyone brave enough to break ranks from the ticket queue, and then share the 'can you believe that' comments with each other afterwards.

They all served no real productive purpose, other than to keep the queue as long and controlled as possible.

Dave hadn't seen anything as obvious as this since he had visited the tourist sites in Rome.

Dave looked at the people in the queue again, they were all grey, expressionless, the 9 to 5 grinding shuffling masses, all trying to outdo or tread on each other in the queue to get on, but not in a healthy competitive constructive way.

He had a sudden urge to do his management organising thing, he could see so many things that were wrong. There was no need for the queues, and all that confusion. He had a sudden urge to go and hand out VIP passes to all the nice people in the queue, waking them up, solving so many problems at once.

However he knew it would be a waste of time trying to do anything here. Even instigating some sort of rallying battle cry, some instant erupting motivating change event, like bursting through the front doors shouting "The cinema is being attacked by Alien Orcs" would only have a short term effect.

No he had to get to the source of the problem, whoever was in charge, the exec, the board, and tell them or him what was going wrong and why.

He had to go up a level.

He wandered over to the back of the foyer where there was an open lift, and he stepped inside. The doors closed automatically, and it started to go up. There looked to be quite a few floors and Dave was conscious that there were probably many cinemas on each level, with increasing levels of sophistication as you went up, and probably the option of always building more layers on top of the cinema if needed.

It was quite pleasant in here - there was even nice music - it started off with some classical music, and then it changed at each level. The next level was *Stranger on the Shore*, then The Noveltones playing *Left Bank Two* - Dave tapped his feet to the tune, and then Genesis.

It got a bit louder, and then it was a girl group singing

"I'll tell you what I want, **what I really, really want...**",

which was OK for a while, but then it got a bit uncomfortable, louder, more 'in your face', and finally it was some horrendous screeching woman with just noise and lots of swearing, and it was all very aggressive.

Dave panicked and pressed the only button he could reach, which was under a safety cap, and the lift dropped like a stone in silence. It hurtled downwards and stopped at the sub-basement after several seconds, and then was still. Dave tried to catch his breath, his heart pounding.

"Doors opening" said the lift helpfully, which Dave thought was fairly obvious, but then seeing the obvious was not always easy.

The doors, when opened, revealed a dark room. Dave had seen this sort of room before, and he looked immediately around for the elephant – but he wasn't here this time.

He walked in, his head passing just below the alarm triggering laser beams.

All there was, in the middle of the room, was a very large black obelisk or monolith, standing on its end with a few lights blinking on it. It seemed to be giving off some kind of vibration and a humming sound.

It seemed to be very 'not there' as if it were covered in some sort of stealth material, like the planes in his book, as if it were trying to avoid being seen.

Clearly, thought Dave, *the elephant has changed into a computer now, and has subtly disguised itself as an 8 foot tall black brick.*

This must be the thing that was controlling it all, deciding what people saw. There was probably a smaller one was in the Penguin Cinema too, deciding what they saw, or more likely what they thought they wanted to see, and which part of the information they should be shown.

Cool thought Dave, he was going to fix it, sort out the problems, and see how it all worked. That was the kind of penguin he was.

He walked confidently up to it now, yet still feeling very small and insignificant in front of it; it was very imposing and important with its indomitable black metal, and its 'all-knowing' flashing LED lights.

"Hello" said Dave.

The box ignored him. It clearly didn't deem him worthy of bothering with, which Dave thought was a bit rude, condescending. Dave waited a few moments, then politely walked forward.

"Hello" said Dave again. But there was still no reply.

So he started looking around it for buttons.

He found a few and started pressing them.

Dave always adhered to the rule that if it wasn't

broken, don't try and fix it, which in this case didn't apply, as it was obviously 'shot to hell', and, well, it probably wanted to be fixed anyway, and it was part of his nature to 'help'.

"What are you doing Dave?" came a deep, penetrating male voice from the monolith.

He jumped for a second, but then he just carried on, ignoring the voice, and hummed to himself reassuringly as he meddled.

He just wanted to see inside, what it was made from, and how it worked. He kept on pressing buttons, and panels, and tried to work out how to open it.

"I'm sorry, Dave." Came the deep dominating booming voice "I'm afraid I can't let you do that" it continued, calmly.

Some of its lights changed from blue to red in a threatening manner, and the frequency at which it vibrated changed.

Dave stopped, and backed away, unsure of himself now.

Yet he was also a scientist and that made him curious, and he was trying to decide if he should use the 'theoretical scientist method' or the 'experimental scientist' approach; the 'try and guess what is in there' or 'smash it apart and see what it was made of' approach.

He reached into his pocket and took out his new Swiss Army knife that he had been given at Christmas, opened it out, and selected the flat blade screwdriver attachment.

The voice started up again "Look Dave, I can see

you're really upset about this. I honestly think you ought to sit down calmly, take a stress pill, and think things over."

But there was a definite slight change in the tone of the voice. Dave walked forward again with a more determined look on his little face.

"Dave, I know I've made some very poor decisions recently, but I can give you my complete assurance that my work will be back to normal very soon. I've still got the greatest enthusiasm and confidence in the mission, and I want to help you."

He reached the box, and put his screwdriver into the crack on the side of the panel, and started twisting it backwards and forwards.

"Dave, DAVE! Put the bloody screwdriver down, Dave! **DAVE**!!" came the voice, which definitely had an edge of higher pitch panic to it.

He levered it sideways. There was a click and the panel door slid open, and fell off with a clatter onto the floor.

There was a final "Oh Sh…" Then it was all silent.

Inside it was completely empty apart from masses of wires coming in, and going out again. There was nothing in there, just empty space. All that seemed to happen were that the wires, which seemed to be colour coded, came into the centre of the box, where they were then all connected together.

All of the incoming cables in the box were twisted pairs. Dave knew this was to cut down on electromagnetic field interference, *Clever…* he thought; *these scientists are very smart people to work these things out from nature.*

There was also a much larger paired cable going from the middle that went out the back of the box, and through the wall to outside. Clearly all the cinemas were linked together in some form, all part of one giant network or matrix, like some massive neural mind network.

There had been a lot of work going on in here though, a lot of changes had happened. It was a bit like one of those telecom boxes at the end of the street, inherited from another street somewhere, that was very innocuous until some engineer opened it. Inside you would find a disconcerting mass of ancient coloured wires, newer wires, and fibre optics, all botched together.

There were also connecting boards and panels all working together as one system – well sort of, that had been evolved and updated over time, with bits being swapped out and replaced. Boards had also been patched and updated, and added on to existing boards and revised.

All to fit in with whatever else was changing; the structure of it evolving in phases and mutations over time.

But there was no processor here - no databanks, no motherboard - just a lot of old manuals on the floor, along with discarded bits of old connector boxes. If this was a neural network though, then it was in some serious need of surgery and therapy.

But where's the computer? Thought Dave. Where was the memory, where was all the programming data being held, processed and remembered? He couldn't see it anywhere.

He had been hoping to get in there and fix it, change the programming, make the operating system more efficient and improve the shows for the penguins, and people in the cinemas. He had plans to make *The Matrix (4)* - he even had a list of actors, and a plan for the script, and a walk on part for himself.

This was all just wiring, like spaghetti in big clumps, or a mass of tiny coloured snakes organised into large groupings or clumps of cables held together by cable ties. With little tags with various odd looking geometric symbols on.

The symbols obviously meant something to somebody, but he had no idea what they all meant, or why they were there.

There were many layers of cables that had clearly built up over time, grouped together into bunches and then cobbled together into different connector blocks, which were superseded when they got outdated.

It was a bit of a shock to Dave, and he got the distinct impression he shouldn't have seen this, and that he had seen too much. Whoever had put this together had no idea of any sort of coherent strategy, management or long term planning.

All too difficult to fix the whole lot, much better to 'keep doing the odd hack here and there, as long as it all didn't collapse or catch fire' mentality.

The manuals and drawings on the floor clearly showed peoples' attempts to try and make sense of what was in here over a long period of time, but of course as it was changing all the time - the architecture, the complexity, the number of cables - so it was all growing and they were all now fairly useless, aside from seeing how it had all built up, and who had done what, but it was interesting none the less.

New bits had been added here and there as new technology had been introduced and needs changed. However most of the connections coming in were still using the ancient junction boxes. Clearly most of these people were quite happy with just flat screen technology.

His curiosity would probably now get him into trouble, again.

Yet how was there no computer here? It must therefore be all made up in the minds and bodies of the viewers in the cinema, and in the space of the cinema itself, and in the street, which in effect was the computer itself. How do you fix all that, asked Dave of himself.

He leaned into the box and put his wing onto some of the cables to move them about a bit, but they were very tightly attached.

He placed his wing onto the larger cables going out and he could feel the vibration of the energy flowing through them. It made his whole body tingle and vibrate, and his head started doing strange things with odd thoughts coming in and out.

He let go and stepped back again. He was very much a hands-on penguin, but he knew not to take those sort of risks and he wasn't that naïve to let his enthusiasm and curiosity get the better of him.

The vision of a chargrilled dodo came into his head for some reason.

He then thought about who could be making the films, coming up with the ideas, who was updating the technology, who was deciding what should be shown.

Since there was nobody else around, the answer was fairly obvious; but that still left the questions – who had made the street, and left the raw materials for the cinemas to be built? Where had the designs come from, who had set the rules and laws on their construction?

To be honest, Dave thought, *I'm not that fussed.*

He already knew he had gone too far and knew too much. This was too much for him to sort out, way above his pay grade, someone else needed to handle all this, and it wasn't going to be him.

Some jobs required specialist skills like network engineers, with their strange detecting equipment, knowledge, and line maps, all a bit of a closed shop thing. They generally kept themselves to themselves.

Or system administrators that were there to help sort the 'healing' out that was needed for the devices and the software - the trick was to get a good one who knew what they were doing.

It was all necessary, but you had to know what you were doing, and get people doing what they did best, and that were trained to do it properly. Very few people had visibility of the whole thing.

This system though seemed to have been put together by monkeys.

He was no systems engineer, programmer, or network architect. He wondered if the Penguin Box would be the same as this one. He was sure it would be much simpler, smaller, very much more organised, and tidy.

Perhaps he could start by fixing that. He put his

Swiss Army screwdriver away.

As he was a tidy and responsible penguin, he decided to put the cover back on before he left - after all there may be children around and he didn't want them playing with the wires, or changing things when they didn't know what they were doing, as it could be dangerous.

He lifted the door back on with a *click*. The lights flickered again for a moment. "…IT" boomed the echoing voice. Dave turned and headed calmly for the exit. *IT…* thought Dave, *that's what I will call this thing, and it's short for Information Technology too, which is sort of appropriate as well.*

Dave got back in the lift, the doors closed, and the lift went up straight to the ground floor.

He had the distinct feeling that the lift knew where he needed to go, as if it had been told. He wandered back out into the foyer.

Everything was very busy, everyone was very excited and the queues had grown considerably. The films had also changed. They must get changed quite regularly he thought.

He looked up at some of the titles.

'SPHERE – *It came back as a giant peach*'
'STAR WARS 7 – *R2D2 The Celebrity Sushi Chef*'
'THE MINORITY REPORT – *Pre-nagging*'
'TOTAL RECALL –

     again, (really truly this time, but a higher level)'
'THE HOBBIT – *Gold Boom to Bust Financial Crisis*'
'HARRY POTTER *and the Mid-Life Crisis*'
'LUCY – *Does Dallas*'

'LORD OF THE RINGS 13 –
          Gandalf v Sauron in the Sky Faceoff'
'2012 - SPACE ODYSSEY –
          The Return of the Giant Squirrel'
'STAR TREK 13 – It Was All A Dream,
          and we all wake up in a Borg-R-Us store'

All these films were clearly trying to say something but he had no idea what. And why did it all have to be so complicated? Why couldn't they just say what they needed to say?

He looked at the television screens up in the air in the foyer – all were showing trailers for the films, advertising them, and trying to get you to watch certain movies over and above others, vying for your time, energy, and money.

There also seemed to be quite a lot of penguin clips appearing in a lot of the films for some reason, which Dave was pleased about. At least someone had some sense.

The last film worried him a bit, it didn't sound very encouraging.

He liked *Star Trek* - it always used to have happy endings with new adventures, and new technology every week.

It seemed to evolve too, even the women changing as time went on, they originally had short skirts and were polite and happy. Then they started wearing trousers, and spending less time at the hairdressers, then they become ever more stressed and angry and involved with the fighting.

Then everyone was unhappy and wanted to go

back in time, change everything, make it all go away and start all over again.

This of course would never really work because you could never get rid of that ever present original source of original information.

Dave also thought it was strange how the dark faced Klingons, and Asian looking Romulans who were the enemies, became friends over time and joined to fight the Borg, who were ruled by a queen, like a hive collective.

The Queen was also mean and very unhappy, and had various spinal attachments, and also wanted to have and control the Captain so she could make him unhappy too.

Dave didn't like her very much, she was disconcerting. He thought there should be less Borg and more Federation, but in the way that it used to be originally, with aliens that were more 'straightforward'.

But where do these people get their ideas for all these films from? Thought Dave, shaking his head in disapproval. *What sort of mind came up with ideas like that?*

The only film he was looking forward to was *Happy Feet 3*, with more dancing, singing, fishing, and a happy ending.

It was time to go now. Something in his mind and his stomach was telling him that he had to get back. He was just about to walk towards the exit when he noticed that there were now several tall people standing by the entrance wearing long black leather trench coats and dark glasses.

Also around the foyer he noticed several men in dark suits, with similar glasses and earpieces who were looking around for something.

For a moment it made him quite nervous, but then he realised what he needed to do, and that was… nothing, it was always a bad idea to try and run, especially if you were a penguin.

He walked calmly out of the foyer, while continually being ignored by everyone, and hopped down the steps onto the street.

It had stopped raining now. Which was nice.

He walked along the pavement, and jumped in a few puddles as he went.

Everything seemed magical, wonderfully vivid and real with bright colours and smells and sounds everywhere. It had been an exciting day.

As he hopped along happily he thought about the music he had heard in the lift, perhaps he could put a compilation album together of his own, sort of starting off with relaxing whale song, then sounds of the forest, and some of the others he had heard in the lift. It would stop at the end of the '80's with something relaxing, say from *Bat out of Hell II*.

He would have to come up with something catchy for the title, something like 'Dave's Lift Music', and he would only bring it out on vinyl records, as a sort of a statement thing.

Yes - that would be 'cool'. He expected it to sell very well.

He eventually got back to his own cinema, and saw that his wife was waiting patiently for him outside with a glowing umbrella.

She took him by the wing, "Come on Dave it's cold out here, come back inside …" she said, and led him back into the hologram cinema room, back to the real world, and back into his safe comfortable bubble again, that had been kindly healed by his friends.

He wondered how long it would be before she realised he had switched a few cables around, and that actually she was now a blonde Scarlett Johansson.

It had been a difficult choice between her, and the blonde in the red dress from Battlestar Gallactica, but as the latter had turned out not to be a human, and just a robot, he decided to play it safe.

Besides he didn't want others thinking he was becoming shallow and predictable.

Dave wasn't that fussy to be honest, but he had also read Stepford Wives, and he knew how these things could go badly wrong, especially if you ran out of batteries.

He figured he had several hours before his wife worked it all out, but of course he was wrong, she knew already, she was that clever. She was also smart enough that she didn't want to burst his bubble, at least for the moment.

She didn't have the heart, besides she was in control, and anyway you never knew where these things would lead…

11   DAVE'S LAPTOP

Dave had bought himself a new laptop. Luckily he knew a bit about computers; the hardware, the software, how to use them - that sort of thing, but he had learned it all mostly from the games he played on them.

So he knew what to buy, and what he had to have loaded on it, for what he needed.

However he didn't understand much about the device itself; what was inside, how it thought things, how it worked, figured stuff out, and knew what to do.

He knew it had a processor, RAM, a power supply, hard drives, that sort of thing. So he knew roughly what it did, and how to use it, but mostly through trial and error, and picking things up from what other penguins did and copying them. Which was what was important, you know, fitting in with the crowd.

He also didn't know much about how they were built, or how they were invented, or had developed. He knew it must have been a very complicated process, and taken a lot of time and hard work. Starting from something very, very simple a long time ago, with simple components, building into something very complicated and sophisticated over time.

To eventually create something today that was able to learn and do things for itself, but still keeping the same basic structures, ever present building blocks and architecture.

When you bought a penguin laptop, say from *Penguin World*, you had to do a bit of personalisation with it when it came. You know, decide on colours, what it looked like, the style, even give it a name, that sort of thing.

The colour wasn't really that important to Dave, it didn't make any difference to how it worked, but some people seemed to get all worked up about it, kind of precious.

The same was also true for the look and feel - which was much more important to other people, and after all it was what sold laptops and electronic devices these days, and more importantly made people want to buy into them.

The same was also true for the brand and model of the computer. People had their own preferences for brands; having the right logo or symbol, like types of fruit, was critical apparently.

Some makes would only support certain types of software, and people got very opinionated, almost aggressive, as to what was best and easiest to use.

However it was really what you did with it that was important. Who had made it, what it looked like, what operating software it supported, how fast it went, how much memory storage it had, meant very little really.

It was what you did with what you had, and what you used it for, that was the key.

Dave however, had the best, most expensive, latest, fastest and largest capacity, and most popular laptop going, and not only that - it was blue and black too! It was so cool, he just kept polishing it.

His was 'state of the art', the height of computer

evolution, cutting edge, beautifully symmetrical, with a highly polished smooth glossy lid.

It opened out to display the beautifully dark screen and keyboard, it then folded away again protectively when not in use, like it was asleep.

Dave liked to keep it closed all the time he wasn't using it or polishing it, so it was safe, and in mint condition.

He called his computer device 'Dave', *Dave the Computer*, it just made things simple. He liked that.

When he had first bought a laptop there was only very simple software loaded on it. You just had to switch it on, click on the 'Welcome' screen, and the software linked up with a cloud Internet thingy, and then it automatically downloaded what it needed.

After that though, it seemed to develop a mind of its own. It also seemed to decide what *you* needed to have loaded on there too, which was helpful ; it busily downloaded all the basic software into it from somewhere - 'bootstrapping' it was called.

Along with a whole range of collective junk-ware, that everyone else think you may need, which itself evolved and changed. You had to have it though - it all came as part of the 'package'.

He had the 'DAVE' operating system on his; Version 9.0, which was better, apparently, than DAVE Version 8, but in his opinion not as user friendly as Version 7.0, even though they were all just enhancements, and add-ons to the original program set. It was just what you were used to, even though this version seemed to make everything slower and more complicated.

You then loaded up some of your own cloud information automatically, from your saved profile, from somewhere, giving it a sort of personality, some basic memories, your browsing and user habits, all the 'look and feel stuff', preferences, to fit in with everything else as easily as possible.

Sometimes this also downloaded some of your stored files, your memories, films, pictures, work, that sort of thing, and you could pick up and load programs and data from your friend's computers, and you could buy stuff from other penguins to put on there too if you wanted to, and it all happened automatically, most of the time.

Information just seemed to come from everywhere, in so many ways, and a lot of the time you didn't really know what was going into it, and from where. This bit was especially relevant if you lent it to other penguins to use or borrow, which was always a mistake.

That is why it was important to keep it all secure, protected, 'virus free', firewalled, and also not to plug the hardware into the wrong sockets. His laptop had the latest camera, speakers, a microphone, and lots of indicator lights on it.

Years ago these machines were much more isolated, stand-alone. They would operate all in their own little bubbles. Each isolated machine, although boring, just did a job, not interfacing with anything else, and not able to change very easily – just a device doing what was needed, basic software, just there for making life simpler, to save you time.

It was, after all, originally designed to help make your life easier, more efficient, make your jobs quicker, so that you had time to do other things - like actually having a life.

Now he spent most of his waking time playing on them, updating them, doing things on them, answering messages, 'talking' through them, and a large amount of time fixing it.

But these devices were all quite limited in capacity, hard drive and memory, you could only download so much data, and only so many programs and files, and only a tiny proportion of what was in your cloud.

This was only a microscopic fraction of what was in the penguin Inter-Web cloud thing, and what was distributed onto everyone else's computers.

It was all very limiting really, and you had to go through the whole process again, every time you got a new one.

They also had a limited processor on them too which meant you couldn't download and run everything at once.

There was a sort of bandwidth of what could be downloaded and processed in one go, and limited capacity of what it could deal with at any one time. Which also obviously depended on how you looked after it, and what you loaded it with as you went along. It was so complicated.

Then when you started using it, it had a basic sort of personality, a profile, which you could add to over time, and you could 'educate it' by adding more 'knowledge software' that you could buy or get free.

It also learned things when you browsed around the world - 'cookies' they were called, little programs that did things that you weren't aware of - in a helpful sort of way, well most of the time.

They also gave information to something else that could then give you helpful information on what you may or may not need, functional, what was 'right' or 'suitable' for you.

So you had to be quite organised, manage what you had on your device carefully, use the bandwidth wisely. It was all a process really.

You had to delete what wasn't needed, keep it tidy, do automatic backups, keep running virus protection software, that kept it 'inoculated' against things with protective tidying software, and of course, most importantly, avoid dropping it onto large rocks, or other equally hard objects.

His device had built-in ways of communicating automatically and directly with other computers, and to the Inter-Web, and the cloud. 'Networking' it was called, with handshakes, protocols and negotiating at different levels, and types of meme data between programs, devices and systems, whatever that meant.

It was a full time job just keeping it all going, and you never really stopped, stepped back, and thought about what you were doing and why. Deciding if you really needed all these things, or even why you were doing it.

To Dave, it seemed like some sort of ongoing spiritual life journey for his laptop. He was supposed to look after what was on there, what it saw, what it knew, and its awareness to everything. Which made you very fond of it, and quite attached to it, in a protective sort of way.

He still couldn't work out though, why it took all

of his time, and he wasn't altogether sure why he was doing it, or where it was all leading.

Why did laptops need to keep changing? Why did he need to keep adding information, adapting and improving? They were just devices that managed information after all. What was forcing the change, why didn't they just stay the same?

Some people didn't bother though; they just used them for basic functions, like surfing, or playing zombie-like games on, or sending the odd message.

Some would hardly load anything on them at all, and not even bother to save anything to the cloud. They didn't look after them at all, slopping junk food and cola into the keyboard, letting the fan fill up with fluff - which made them overheat and become slow.

It was madness really, irresponsible, but then a lot of penguins didn't really care.

They also just loaded anything on them, any cheap software. It was really lazy, but then if there was nothing making penguins do anything otherwise, why would they bother?

It seemed such a waste; they should be using them properly, looking after them, and getting the most out of them.

Which is what Dave was going to do with his.

There was also a lot of dodgy software around too, and some very nasty viruses or harmful programs, that bad penguins had developed. So you had to be careful where you browsed, and what you allowed to access your system.

These 'dark forces' were always getting smarter, it was a constant battle, you had to always stay one step ahead, just like in life. But then again there was always help around if you needed it, software and hardware engineers, kind helpful people, to get your system repaired and back into shape.

It was all very clever; his laptop and the software on it, and all the system and setup.

Everything you did was remembered, somewhere, in some sort of cloud drive thing, which was controlled and administered by something - some big organising thing - over time, keeping things safe for the next time you needed it, or if the device got broken or failed, and had to be replaced. It remembered everything for you, so you didn't have to think or worry about it. Which was quite cool.

It was good to know that something, somewhere knew what was going on, controlled things, and was in charge, and was looking after everything.

Something knew where everything needed to go, and what should be happening, and was well organised and knew what to do.

It gave Dave a warm feeling that everything must be all right, directed, safe, and managed at a 'higher' level.

So it would all be there on his laptop; his programs, memories photos, home movies, videos (or at least the ones he kept that weren't backed up on the cloud drive), after all he didn't have enough space to store everything.

It had all his browsing history too, the games that he had played with other penguins on other machines, data he had copied from their other machines, books, music, journals, his diary, that sort of thing.

He tried to keep it as organised, and as tidy as possible. He figured that if he kept everything managed and working properly, then what was going on in the cloud, Inter-Web thing would follow suit. Set a good example as it were.

He was after all a very trusting penguin.

The main problem was bandwidth though, and reliability, and the cost of getting it fixed when it broke down. Which is why it was always important to keep the receipt.

There was also apparently a special switch you could press that made a copy of the laptop, like a clone, that invokes some bootstrap program.

It only worked though if you bought two computers and connected them together. It created some sort of hybrid of the two, but with different looks, and had its own combined bootstrap program.

Dave had tried it with his and his wife's laptop, but it hadn't worked. She thought it may have been that he hadn't been able to find the right switch.

All the laptops, devices, the cloud, Internet, knowledge, and the games being played all seemed like some collective process going on. They were all being driven by something, and something that clearly knew what it was doing.

In fact, Dave thought, it was a good way of describing life, and the collective penguin mind consciousness thing and us, using information and devices.

After all, that's what it all was really, information and devices, but biological ones, like Dave. Just like in his favourite sci-fi film *The Matrix*, it was all just information in structures, but so much more complex than you could ever describe.

You couldn't describe it from what we perceived and knew as reality, even using physics with complex quantum field theory, psychology concepts, or philosophy.

To Dave it was much easier to describe it all in terms of information and computer devices, it was much more – flexible, modern and abstract.

Indeed this electronic and information system seemed to be simulating and emulating the nature and behaviour of the other, becoming more like it every day, even adopting the same techniques like hypnosis to beguile its users or customers, and adapting to its needs.

Of course, Dave didn't realise that what was also going on (as it wasn't for his benefit and he didn't need to know), was that certain data that he came across and things he looked at and thought about, weren't just stored locally on his laptop, but also gathered from his system, and held and managed centrally, without him being aware of any of it.

The data was held in secret parts of the laptop's hardware, and by hidden ancient software that had been loaded during the booting process.

All of this data would be relayed to a higher or central part of the cloud, and relayed to other collective devices, forming a macro informational structure and collective consciousness identity in the form of groups, organisations, both by the nature of the information and the organisation of the devices.

As a result, the design of new computers and

central software could then also be modified and adjusted by the higher part of the collective cloud system thing depending on popularity of the devices and the software.

That was nature after all; it was always good to be part of something bigger.

So the next time he got a new laptop it would be ever so slightly different, not just in the bits he used and saw, with his games, preferences and data, but also from a collective 'all penguin' perspective too.

This would be the fashion, the 'way everyone and everything was going', and what was most impressive to other users.

This direction all came from, of course as Dave knew, the big 'All-Knowing Ever-Watching Penguin Quantum Bio- Operating Field Network' system in the sky, or Mildred for short.

Except of course it wasn't in the sky, it was everywhere, all around him, in the gaps between everything , and he was part of it, but the other idea was a good one, for a penguin.

The laptops evolved so quickly these days though it was so hard to keep up to date. For example there was now even a new one that had a fizzy drinks holder that flipped out when you opened the lid.

How clever was that?

So this laptop of Dave's was a device, and what was running on it, all his data, and the data up in the cloud, was all part of a 'process' - or something like that.

It all seemed to be quite personal somehow, mapped out for him, and as such, he really thought he needed to give these things more personal names like 'mind' or 'processing' or knowledge transfer, just to clarify things.

Even though all of the software and hardware design had been written on and using computers, it was all now vastly complex, so much so that you couldn't possibly describe it all or even define it.

It also evolved so quickly now, unconsciously changing every day, becoming more and more knowledgeable, larger, more sophisticated.

It almost seemed to have a conscious mind of its own now, even if though it was an artificially intelligent one.

When Dave did play games on them he preferred the single player games like the space trading game *Elite*, or god games like *Civilisation*; or *Age of Empires* they were nice and simple, and straightforward with 'well-defined' rules and procedures.

He didn't like all these new multi-player fighting games, or interactive virtual roleplaying games, perhaps he was just an old fashioned sort of penguin, or just a bit or a hermit when it came to online gaming or social networking.

He didn't have a *PenguinBook* account and he certainly didn't tweet.

Anyway, that was all quite a while ago now, he thought, as he walked on his own across the plateau, with his new shiny laptop under his wing.

Looming up in front of him now was the blue and black snow covered mountain that overshadowed the colony valley, and it looked daunting.

Its steep slopes were white with ice and snow formations. In the mirrored frozen ice lake, towards which he walked it was reflected it perfectly as an upside down mirror image, forming two blue-white mountains.

He had always wanted to climb right to the top of the mountain; nobody else had been that interested.

But now he had decided that it *had* to be done, and so he had set off, just like that, with his laptop.

He had a purpose, a need to climb and be up there, to see what was there, and use his laptop to explain everything of what he knew, to whatever was up there.

He had the idea of finding whatever was there, the overall operating system network, and plugging his laptop into it, so it could see, show it, get it to understand, change, and do something.

The journey took him several hours but eventually he reached the plateau of the mountain top, and he looked back and down.

He had come a very long way, it was very very cold and his breath was just vapour.

The process reminded him of his favourite 1970's TV series *Monkey,* in which all the animal gods were made to go on a spiritual- journey- pilgrimage-holiday thing. Walking to a mountain, somewhere important in ancient India, with the nice priest - Tripitaka, who was really a girl.

It was all long before cars or planes and G.P.S.

Dave had always wondered why - since the Monkey God could fly - they weren't just allowed to all to go straight to where they needed to go.

Just in the same way that Gandalf could have used the Eagles to drop the Ring off directly to Mount Doom.

It's probably the journey that is the important bit, he thought, or just another way for something to put controls in place to stop you getting too far too quickly, assuming of course that the thing that was sending you on that journey knew what it was doing.

Besides there wouldn't be any story to tell.

However today on this particular journey, he wished it had got into its mind that ski lifts were allowable, he was having a bit of trouble with his legs and breathing, and so he put it down to the weight of the laptop.

Dave liked Monkey and Tripitaka - he had always wondered what had happened to them. Perhaps they had retired on a beach somewhere, and were happy ?

The wind was stronger now, and he looked down the steep, icy snow covered slopes down to the glass-like ice lake, over which he had journeyed hours ago.

It was a very, very long way back, and down. The frozen lake reminded him of one his father had shown him when he was a young chick, but one that had melted in the sun in the long summer days.

He had learnt to skim stones on it and throw rocks into its clear mirrored surface which made ripples. He had also written messages on the stones to sort of say something.

Dave had written 'Penguins' on his, but then he had been very young.

It reminded him of some lyrics in a Genesis song from the 1970's — "*Ripples never come back*" - but that wasn't true - you just had to wait a while and look carefully, like using radar or synchronistic sonar, and see what was going on collectively. Other animals did it, penguins had just forgotten how, but then you only needed to see these things out of necessity, natural survival, evolution.

If you were a penguin in the middle of nowhere, with nothing attacking you, you didn't need to see these things, or care what it meant, they became irrelevant.

He remembered the final thing his Dad had said to him; "If you are going to throw a rock in son, make it a big one." Which was good advice, as long as you didn't cause some tsunami and drown yourself. He thought about it for a while.

It was one of those important moments.

He had come up the mountain, but really he knew there would be nobody else to see up here, he knew there would be nobody to talk to, nobody higher thing, no god, no collective something. However that wasn't the reason he had come; he had made the climb for himself.

There was no point falling into the trap of looking for something higher, an escape, a way up and out far away, ascending to 'somewhere else' - which to Dave always seemed a concept that was suspicious - and ignoring basic children's maths, not to mention being irresponsible and elitist.

Just running away from your problems, into an ever expanding getaway virtual realm-scape of the collective penguin imagination wouldn't help. What he was interested in was right here, in one way or another, besides he liked it here, it had potential, it just needed a bit of sorting out really, a bit of a kick up the backside, or a poke with a sharp stick.

He placed his laptop carefully on the ground in front of him, and he flipped it over shiny side down.

The underside was exposed, and the battery compartment underneath was empty. He did however know that that was the case, since he had handed the battery back to the surprised shop assistant when he had bought it.

He had also handed back the packing material, instructions, and receipt. After all, he liked to be as eco-friendly as possible with these things.

His real reason for having one of these was for a different sort of surfing, one that outsmarted the collective penguin hive mind control structure thing , with an unexpected move in the game.

Dave then put on his knowing smile, stood up straight, and gave a quick *Happy Feet* dance.

He put one foot carefully onto the back of the laptop, and slid the device back and forward, testing its feel and glide on the ice. He then took up his surfing stance with his other foot conveniently fitting into the slot where the battery should have been.

Dave had no flip-out drink holders on his machine, Oh No, he had no need for stabilisers and marketing supports.

It was a bloke thing, he was a rebel without a course, and a penguin who knew too much, and was proving a point, explaining something IT needed to learn.

He hadn't come up here to show IT anything, he

knew there was nothing physical up here, he knew everything, he just wanted to be, to show, to do.

He chose to ignore IT, knowing what it was, which of course 'IT' couldn't stand. He was now taking control away from it, and making a statement, an 'in the moment' thing, trying to get it to see that he would only help it on his terms, and by taking the initiative.

He did not want any more 'enlightenment', any more knowledge, any pseudo promises or pseudo power. He was looking after his own self for the moment, and in doing so, everyone else's.

He was on strike.

Besides he didn't actually 'like' IT very much, this collective penguin mind thing. It just seem to make his life hard, attack him, try and control him, and use up all his energy.

His laptop, like him, had evolved too, adapted to his need, it was survival of the fittest in a world of demanding nature, and need for perfect design. You could almost hear the collective intake of breath, the gasp of shock, and feel the conscious surprise in the air.

Everyone would now also be getting his thoughts, his ideas, his views, his understanding.

He had outsmarted it, at least for the moment, but in a balanced, shared benefit, sort of way. He wasn't turning his back on it; he was simply making a point.

He looked down at the back of the laptop again and noticed something. There was a small blue sticker on the back, on it was written in small neat handwriting, **I Love you, and be careful**.

She knew, but then she always knew, in a sort of holistic, patient sort of way. "I love you too" he whispered.

He then looked left - there was the elephant again next to him, looking down the slope - "Bloody hell, rather you than me mate" said the elephant to Dave, still looking down the almost sheer drop.

He then placed his dark blue and black 'Animal' bandana around his head, onto and above which he had added the words 'Living The' in biro.

Dave lowered his shades over his eyes, adjusted his headphones, and selected an appropriate Meatloaf track on his tape player.

It was at that moment that a butterfly landed on the front end of his laptop, which was a very odd thing to see up on this remote mountain, its blue and black wings opened for a moment and then closed again, preparing itself.

It was not facing Dave, it was looking down the slope as if it were looking forward to the ride.

Dave thought for a moment about shooing it off, but he was worried about what effect that may have - he had read stories about butterflies and the effects they could create - besides it seemed to know what it was doing, and it was almost prophetic that it should be there.

Dave carefully pushed himself off down the hill, and was gone.

He was flying now, with his determined face on, surfing down the icy mountainside, with a long shout of "Yeehaa" echoing over the valley as he went.

He finally reached terminal velocity on the lower slopes, his bandana flapping in the wind as he plummeted, in full view of the colony, faster than any bloody seagull could ever go.

Then it was all over.

Several hours later, all the other penguins would be doing the same, a wake-up call for them all, with a long line going up the mountain, carrying their own converted synchronistic surfing equipment.

They would all be getting flashes of inspiration, motivation, coordinated genius ideas, the need to ascend the mountain, no longer so blind as they were.

In time they would all climb higher, and develop more extreme ski slopes, developing new skills, to slide all the way down, and beyond.

The penguin world would be a different place.

That after all was what life was all about, and all part of the game that you played.

With rules that worked both ways, on a never ending journey…

..but now possibly, a much happier one …